The Best **Clarinet** Book Ever.

Selected and edited by **Emma Coulthard**

Chester Music
(A division of Music Sales Limited)
14/15 Berners Street,
London W1T 3LJ

Contents

Twinkle twinkle little star

Traditional
arr. Emma Coulthard

Anglaise

English, 18th century
arr. Emma Coulthard

Zum Gali Gali

Israeli song
arr. Emma Coulthard

The Lonely Goatherd
from *The Sound of Music*

Richard Rogers
arr. Emma Coulthard

Swing Low Sweet Chariot
& Nobody Knows De Trouble I See

Spirituals
arr. Emma Coulthard

Scarborough Fair

English folk song
arr. Emma Coulthard

Minuet

James Hook, Op. 37 No. 2
arr. Emma Coulthard

Tempo di minuetto

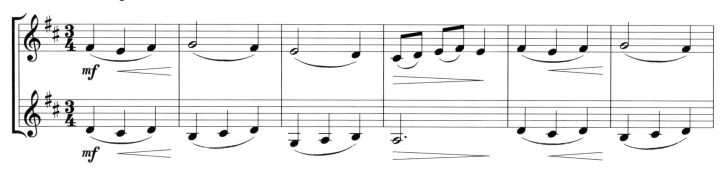

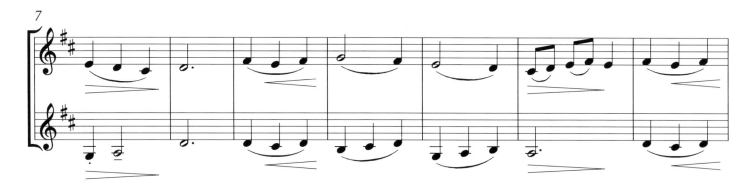

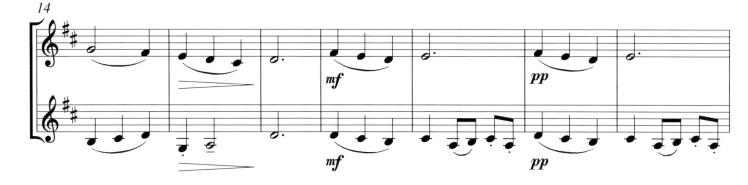

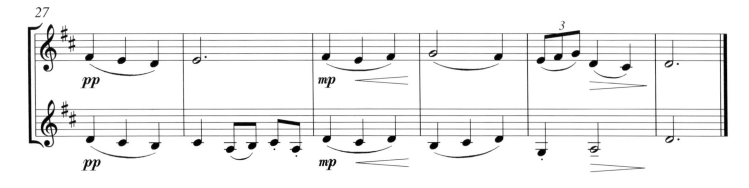

Chim Chim Cher-ee
from *Mary Poppins*

Richard M. Sherman &
Robert B. Sherman
arr. Emma Coulthard

That Sounds So Beautiful
from *The Magic Flute*

Wolfgang Amadeus Mozart
arr. Wilhelm Popp

Theme from *The New World Symphony*

Antonín Dvorák
arr. Emma Coulthard

Happy Birthday

Mildred Hill and Patty Hill
arr. Michael McCartney

Supercalifragilisticexpialidocious
from *Mary Poppins*

Richard M. Sherman &
Robert B. Sherman
arr. Emma Coulthard

Menuetto and Trio

Carl Stamitz, Op. 27

* All trills are optional.

Simple Gifts

Traditional
arr. Emma Coulthard

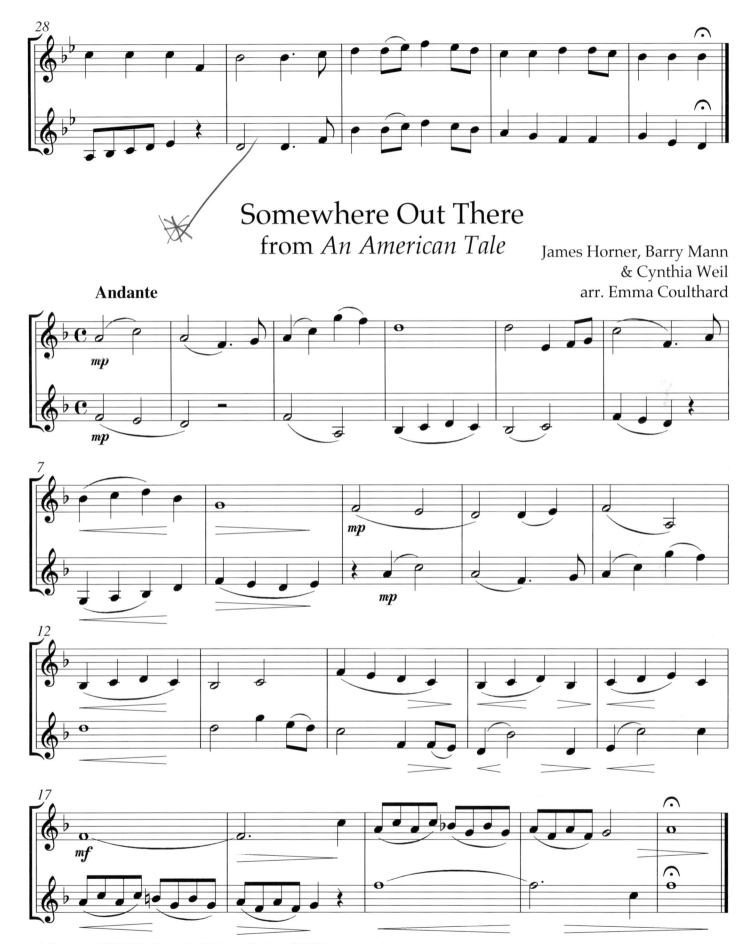

Somewhere Out There
from *An American Tale*

James Horner, Barry Mann
& Cynthia Weil
arr. Emma Coulthard

Andante

Ev'rybody Wants To Be A Cat
from *The Aristocats*

Al Rinker
arr. Emma Coulthard

Greensleeves

English folk song
arr. Emma Coulthard

Andante

Round Dance
from *For Children*

Béla Bartók
arr. Emma Coulthard

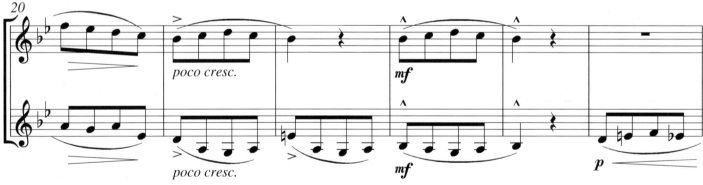

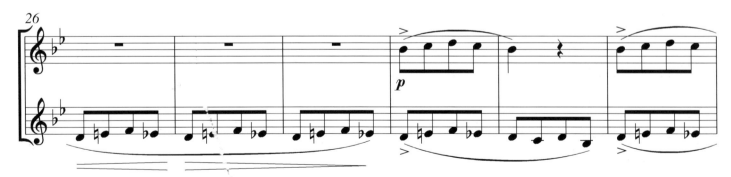

Two Little Pieces
1. A Sad Tale

Dmitri Kabalevsky
arr. Emma Coulthard

Lento e poco pesante

molto lento

2. Country Dance

Evening Prayer
from *Hansel and Gretel*

Engelbert Humperdinck
arr. Michael McCartney

The Last Rose of Summer

Irish folk song
arr. Emma Coulthard

Rondo

Allegretto

François Devienne

Waltz

Mauro Giuliani, Op. 57 No. 5
arr. Emma Coulthard

Tempo di valse ♩ = 140

My Favourite Things
from *The Sound of Music*

Richard Rodgers
arr. Emma Coulthard

Hornpipe
from *Water Music*

George Frideric Handel
arr. Emma Coulthard

Stop!

Victoria Adams, Emma Bunton,
Melanie Brown, Melanie Chisholm,
Geri Halliwell, Andy Watkins & Paul Wilson
arr. Emma Coulthard

Mamma Mia!

Benny Andersson,
Björn Ulvaeus & Stig Anderson
arr. Emma Coulthard

Spring

John Buckley

32

Lento

Igor Stravinsky
arr. Emma Coulthard

Allegro

Igor Stravinsky
arr. Emma Coulthard

Andante cantabile
from *String Quartet no. 1*

Peter Ilyich Tchaikovsky, op. 11
arr. Michael McCartney

Contents

IS THIS THE REAL LIFE? IS THIS JUST FANTASY?

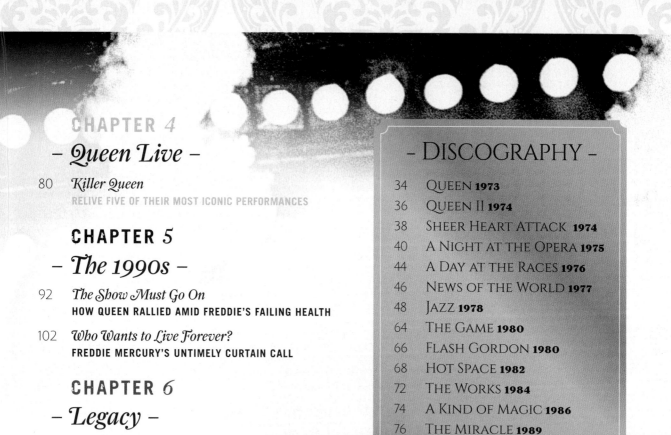

CHAPTER 1
– Early Years –

IS THIS THE REAL LIFE? IS THIS JUST FANTASY?

FREDDIE MERCURY

THE GREATEST ROCK FRONTMAN WHO EVER STALKED A STAGE. NO ARGUMENTS. NO CONTEST

How do you define an icon as glittering as the late Freddie Mercury? With difficulty, given that this sadly departed genius was so much more than the sum of his parts.

The bare facts are that Farrokh Bulsara, as no one called him apart from his parents, was born in Zanzibar on 5 September 1946 and died on 24 November 1991 in London. In those 45 years he became many things: a songwriter, a performer, a lover, an aesthete, a sybarite, and – perhaps inadvertently – an advocate for equal rights, whether that meant in gender politics or elsewhere. Never a father or a husband, he plunged his passion into his music, both with Queen and as a solo artist, facing down endless prejudice along the way.

We often picture Freddie in his trademark white singlet or black leather outfit, with or without his famous moustache – and reasonably so, since those images have been so widely seen – but the fact is that there were many, many incarnations of Freddie. There's the smiling boarding-school kid from Zanzibar; the struggling student, fighting his family tradition and British racism at college; the shy nascent pop singer in the early Queen; the obscure glam-rocker Larry Lurex; and the first flowerings of extroversion as his public profile took hold.

There's the world-class songwriter who wrote 'Killer Queen', 'We Are the Champions', 'Don't Stop Me Now' and a little ditty called 'Bohemian Rhapsody'; the king of Live Aid who held millions of people in the palm of his hand; the master behind all those drug-laced parties; the pale, gaunt man who faced down AIDS in his final years; and over and above all those personalities, the brilliant, affectionate version of Freddie delivered by Rami Malek in the *Bohemian*

Rhapsody movie in 2018, which may well end up being the dominant image of him in most people's minds after all.

The truth is that Freddie was all those characters, and more that we will never hear about: the reality is that he was a private individual who chose carefully to whom, and how much, he revealed of himself. Just one tragic aspect of his early death is that we never got to see

what else he had to offer. How many other personalities would he have presented to the world if he hadn't been taken decades before his time?

We remember him as a unique man, who gave us the gift of his exquisite talent as a member of this similarly unique group of individuals. Don't be sad that Freddie died; be happy that he lived at all. ♛

BRIAN MAY

WHAT DO YOU GET IF YOU CROSS AN ASTRONOMICAL ACADEMIC WITH A GUITAR GENIUS?

Q ueen defied accepted rock music wisdom in many ways, but one important way in which the group was unconventional was in its pairing of singer and guitarist. The Rolling Stones had Jagger and Keef; The Who had Daltrey and Townshend; Aerosmith had Tyler and Perry; Guns N' Roses had Axl and Slash. These were pairs of toxic twins, leader and wingman combined, a professional duo of destruction.

Freddie Mercury and Brian May were never like that. Queen's singer was hellbent on highbrow pleasure and lowbrow debauchery, for sure, but May occupies a wholly different plane to the aforementioned guitar-slingers. An intellectual who loves heavenly bodies and endangered wildlife with equal commitment, May was born on 19 July 1947 and is as far from the stereotype of the boorish rocker as it is possible to be. In fact, how he – along with the similarly unassuming John Deacon – came to be in one of the most theatrical rock bands of all time is something of a mystery.

As a student, May played with Roger Taylor in the band Smile, which transformed into Queen in 1970 and, as we'll see, became famous within a year. Wielding a home-made guitar called the Red Special, he delivered crystal-clear, super-melodic guitar parts with a specific, identifiable tone that blew listeners' minds. You know when it's May playing: there's something about his string-bends, and the ice-cold flurries of notes that he plays, which don't just sound like Queen: they *are* Queen.

As for his recorded catalogue, where do you start? Quite aside from the albums May has released as a solo artist, some of Queen's most-loved songs came from the pen of the rock'n'roll doctor. 'We Will Rock You', 'I Want It All', 'Fat Bottomed Girls', 'Flash', 'Hammer to Fall', 'Save Me', 'Who Wants to Live Forever' and 'The Show Must Go On' are just some of them.

After Freddie died in 1991, Queen's first imperial phase was clearly over, but May and Taylor did the right thing by continuing to keep the brand alive. When the time was right to fully resurrect Queen, the audience was waiting. Outside his custodianship of the band, May received a CBE in 2005 for services to the music industry and for charity work; he earned his PhD in astrophysics from Imperial College London two years later; and he passionately campaigns against fox hunting and the culling of badgers.

There's no one quite like him – and you'll enjoy learning more, as we move on, about the life of Brian. ⚓

ROGER TAYLOR

MOST DRUMMERS DON'T SING, COMPOSE HUGE HITS AND SQUIRE A LEGION OF GROUPIES – BUT MOST DRUMMERS AREN'T ROGER TAYLOR

The drums are the heartbeat of any guitar-heavy band, and we can all name a dozen Queen songs that boast a huge drum performance – but the great thing about this band, and indeed their drummer, is that their softer, subtler songs also have a perfect drum track. The way that Roger Taylor plays to suit a given song is nothing short of miraculous… and let us not forget his unearthly vocal skills, too.

Born on 26 July 1949, Roger Meddows Taylor was born in King's Lynn, Norfolk, where he had an early brush with Queen Elizabeth, who was visiting the hospital's maternity ward at the time. He and his family moved to Truro, Cornwall, and by the age of seven he was playing the ukulele in a school band, later picking up the guitar. At 15, he joined a rock band called The Reaction, switching to drums after realising that they suited his talents better. His early heroes were Keith Moon of The Who and Mitch Mitchell of The Jimi Hendrix Experience, which would account for the heavier end of his drumming technique.

The future rock star was nearly a dentist, having begun to study the subject at the London Hospital Medical College in 1967, but he soon switched to biology, graduating from East London Polytechnic instead. However, rock stardom eclipsed either subject, and as Queen's star rose, Taylor rose with it, writing many all-time classics. Three of their UK chart-toppers were his solo or joint compositions: 'These Are the Days of Our Lives', 'Innuendo' and 'Under Pressure'. He also composed the hits 'Radio Ga Ga', 'A Kind of Magic', 'Heaven for Everyone', 'Breakthru' and 'The Invisible Man' and was the main writer behind the strutting 'One Vision'.

It helped that Taylor was a guitarist as well as singer and drummer, leading

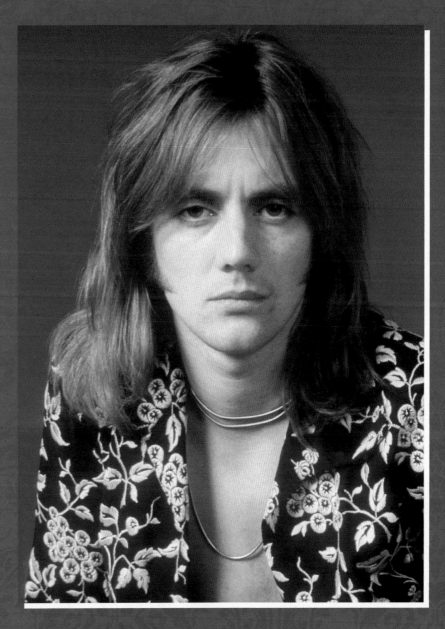

to his status as creative collaborator extraordinaire with a wide range of musicians – Bon Jovi, Eric Clapton, Robert Plant, Roger Waters, Elton John, Gary Numan, Roger Daltrey, Phil Collins, Genesis and Foo Fighters among them. He's also a producer, having helmed recordings by Jimmy Nail, Magnum and others.

All this, and a solo artist, too: Taylor sometimes performed in his own side project, The Cross, in the late 80s and early 90s. As a frontman who sings and plays guitar, Taylor is just as accomplished as when he is behind the kit – making him a rare musician indeed. You can forget all the old drummer jokes when he's around… ♛

JOHN DEACON

'DEACY' IS THE MYSTERY OF QUEEN: THE QUIET ONE
WHO WENT COMPLETELY SILENT. WHAT HAPPENED?

T here is a truth universally acknowledged in rock bands, which is that the singer is an extrovert, the guitarist is desperate for attention, the drummer is a moron, and the bassist is the quiet one who avoids the spotlight. In the case of Queen, only two of these four stereotypes apply, but they apply to the absolute maximum.

The basic facts reveal that John Deacon was just another everyman like the rest of us, at least until Queen took off commercially. He was born in Leicester on 19 August 1951, and his family later moved to the nearby small town of Oadby. He was a clever kid, sailing through his grammar school exams and becoming an electronics geek as a teenager. He put that talent to good use in later years, building the 'Deacy' guitar amplifier for use in Queen.

By 1965, Deacon was playing guitar in a school band, The Opposition, and switched to bass the following year. That group went nowhere, like most school bands, and he went to Chelsea College in London in '69 to study electronics. Two years later he auditioned for Freddie Mercury, Brian May and Roger Taylor and joined Queen.

Bass guitar was his instrument, and he played it with gobsmacking taste and precision, but Deacon's bigger talent was arguably his knack for writing world-class songs such as 'You're My Best Friend', which he wrote for his wife Veronica. See also 'I Want to Break Free' – economical, unselfish songwriting that resonated with millions of people.

As a bass player, he was a master of simplicity. Look at 'Another One Bites the Dust' and 'Under Pressure', both massive hits which begin with a huge bass part that is the songs' best-known feature. Without that bass part, there's really no song, in both cases.

After Freddie's death in 1991, Deacon seemed to have lost all desire not just to be in Queen but to be a regular working musician. He hasn't said much on the subject apart from the oft-quoted "There is no point carrying on; it is impossible to replace Freddie" from *Bassist* magazine in '96. May and Taylor rarely have contact with him any more, the odd business-related email aside.

With the current resurgence in Queen's popularity thanks to 2018's *Bohemian Rhapsody* biopic, you'd wonder if Deacon might show up for a celebratory drink with May and Taylor – but he was nowhere to be seen. Who knows where he was? Perhaps relaxing on his sofa in Putney, watching it on TV and sipping a cup of tea. ♛

DOING ALL RIGHT

Freddie, John, Roger and Brian pictured backstage at the Uris Theatre, New York, in May 1974 while they were the support act for Mott The Hoople.

These Are the Days of Our Lives

STUDENT DAYS, ROCK'N'ROLL AND
NAKED AMBITION: LET'S MEET THE
MEN WHO WOULD BE QUEEN

WORDS *Joel McIver*

H as there ever been a more unusual, or more
iconic, quartet in rock than Queen? After all, they
boasted a flamboyant, insecure singer; a steadfast,
intellectual guitarist; a solid, reliable bassist; and a
pretty, falsetto-singing drummer. Led Zeppelin may have been
more into amped-up blues and folk, Black Sabbath may have
pioneered occult heavy metal – but no one pressed a range of
aesthetic buttons quite like the early Queen.

For that reason, it's hard to imagine the group being made
up of anyone other than Freddie Mercury, Brian May, John
Deacon and Roger Taylor – but when we take their early
history into account, it becomes apparent that the lineup
could have been rather different. The musicians who crossed
paths with the fabulous foursome, but who walked away or
were 'let go' before fame came calling, must have regretted
their decisions once Queen became stars. →

TOP LEFT A childhood photo of Freddie during his time at St Peter's School in Panchgani, India, where he formed his first band called The Hectics.

LEFT The members of Smile in August 1969, from left to right: Bruce Sanderson, Paul Humbertone, Brian May (sitting on bonnet), Pete Edmunds, Tim Staffell, Clive Armitage and Paul Fielder.

ABOVE Freddie pictured in 1969 at Ealing Art College, where he studied graphic art and design.

On the other hand, Queen's beginnings were so humble that no one could have predicted their future success. In the late Sixties, university bands were so common – and let's face it, often so mundane – that few of them looked particularly promising, and that definitely applies to the pre-Queen groups in which our heroes took their first steps into the limelight.

Brian May had been strumming away on his Red Special guitar since 1963, and formed a band called 1984 – after George Orwell's novel – a year later. A bassist, Dave Dilloway, and a singer, Tim Staffell, joined May in this band, although both May and Staffell switched to a new group called Smile when they became university students, with Staffell taking up bass. A keyboard player called Chris Smith joined them, as did a young, hotshot drummer called Roger Taylor

after May advertised on a college notice board for a 'Mitch Mitchell/Ginger Baker type' drummer.

As Staffell, in some ways the catalyst for Queen, remembered in a 2021 interview with *Bass Player* magazine, "In our band, 1984, I was the lead singer and harp player, although on rare occasions when Brian had to miss a gig, I stood in on electric guitar. When we first mooted the notion of Smile, it was a given that I would play bass – but it wasn't that I showed any particular aptitude for the instrument."

He added that there was genuine originality in Smile ("As a trio, it was possible to think outside the box and play around with the musical dynamic. Roger and I weren't a conventional rhythm section per se: we created a fairly unique platform for Brian's guitar and our harmonies to float on") and also that

times were hard, financially speaking. "Equipment was based on affordability and availability," he explained. "In those days, local government would give a student a grant to attend college – and if you were suitably frugal, you could just about stretch to a guitar and an amp alongside college expenses."

By 1969, Staffell had become friends with a fellow student, Freddie Bulsara, while both were attending Ealing Art College in West London, where Freddie did a year studying fashion design before switching to graphic art and design. Freddie also knew Taylor, running a stall in Kensington Market with the drummer, and was a fan of Smile: he even asked Staffell if he could join the band as their lead singer, but the former was unwilling to step aside.

Staffell later recalled a particularly fiery opening slot, saying, "Both 1984

> ## A full reshuffle came when May and Taylor asked Freddie to join them

and Smile supported Jimi Hendrix. I don't recall the gig very well: we shared a dressing room, Jimi asked me the way to the stage, but that's about it!"

Despite these promising signs, a turning point came in 1970 when Staffell quit Smile, having grown tired of the band's flirtation with hard rock when he preferred soul and R&B. "After 18 months of Smile, and supporting the likes of Yes, T. Rex and Free, I was getting dissatisfied," he later explained, "partly because I was falling out of love with heavy rock, and partly because I was networking with people who were great improvisers, jazzers, country pickers and ethnic musicians, and I was developing a real sense of inadequacy with my own efforts. The catalyst for it was that I also wanted to write, and not the kind of material which would have suited Smile."

Keyboardist Smith had left the group the previous year, so a full reshuffle came when May and Taylor asked Freddie to join them. Fortunately, he already had form as a singer: in 1969, he had played with a Liverpool-based band called Ibex, which later renamed itself Wreckage. After that, he joined an Oxford band, Sour Milk Sea, although this group lasted no longer than early 1970. Taylor knew Freddie was a good laugh, later saying "Back then, I didn't really know him as a singer – he was just my mate. My crazy mate! If there was fun to be had, Freddie and I were usually involved."

Taylor's friend Mike Grose also signed up as bassist, and the first gig for the Freddie-fronted group came on 27 June 1970 in Truro, Cornwall, after which the new singer suggested a name change

to Queen. There was some resistance to the idea, slang associated with gay people being subject to suspicion in the prejudiced Seventies, but Freddie insisted that "It's wonderful, dear, people will love it" and so the band was renamed. He later explained, "It's very regal, obviously, and it sounds splendid. It's a strong name, very universal and immediate. I was certainly aware of the gay connotations, but that was just one facet of it."

At the same time, he adopted the stage name Freddie Mercury, inspired by a line from their song 'My Fairy King' that →

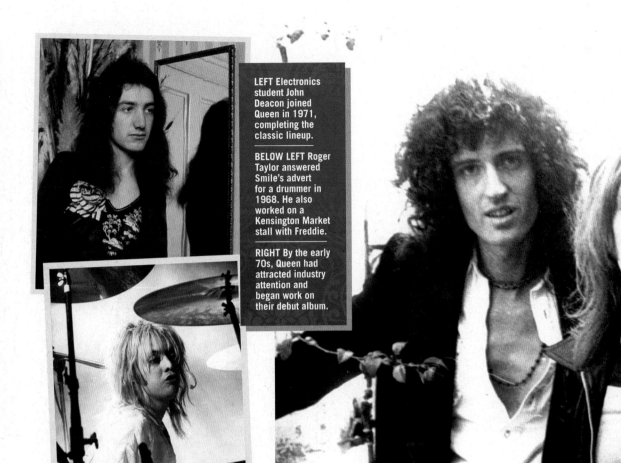

LEFT Electronics student John Deacon joined Queen in 1971, completing the classic lineup.

BELOW LEFT Roger Taylor answered Smile's advert for a drummer in 1968. He also worked on a Kensington Market stall with Freddie.

RIGHT By the early 70s, Queen had attracted industry attention and began work on their debut album.

> **66 Freddie came up with Queen's logo – or more accurately, their coat of arms 99**

ran: "Mother Mercury, look what they've done to me."

Now with a more professional, confrontational image and an alter ego for their singer to inhabit, Queen started to attract attention, especially when a debut London gig came about on 18 July. Along with a few original songs, they played rock'n'roll covers by artists such as Cliff Richard and The Shadows, which we may regard as vintage but were only a few years old at the time. Producer John Anthony saw potential in the pummelling sound of Mercury, May and Taylor – but he also felt that Grose was the wrong bassist for the job.

Perhaps noting this, Grose decided not to stay on, and was replaced by former Crushed Butler bassist Barry Mitchell, who stayed until January 1971, when he in turn was replaced by Doug Bogie for two gigs. Were Queen doomed to a succession of temporary bass players?

Enter John Deacon, who made up for the here-today, gone-later-today nature of his predecessors by remaining on board permanently. After leaving his teenage band The Opposition (later called The Art), Deacon was looking for a gig, having enrolled as a student of electronics at Chelsea College in London. He attended an early Queen show but was less than smitten by the

fledgling rockers: however, after a single gig by his own band, Deacon, he saw the light and auditioned for Taylor and May, having met them at a disco. Once accepted into the ranks, he played his debut gig with Queen at the glamorously titled College of Estate Management in Kensington in June.

The group's music at this point is probably best described as guitar-driven rock with piano and progressive elements, as well as a camp sense of

humour. Freddie often talked about his love of Led Zeppelin, but also said that Queen "have more in common with Liza Minnelli than Led Zeppelin. We're more in the showbiz tradition than the rock'n'roll tradition." Combine those elements and you have the first steps into Queen's phenomenal music – although this meant little until they could secure a producer, a studio album and a label to release it.

In the interim, Freddie put his graphic design skills to good use, coming up with Queen's logo – or more accurately, their coat of arms. The design incorporates the zodiac signs of all four members: a pair of lions for Leo (Deacon and Taylor) and a crab that signified Cancer (May), and he also threw in two fairies for Virgo (Freddie himself). There's also a crown and a phoenix, and all in all, it's a wonderful, extravagant piece of art.

Things soon began to move along nicely. A promoter called Ken Testi persuaded Charisma Records to stump up a decent sum of money – £25,000, over £400,000 today – as an advance, but Queen actually turned them down, a bold move for a young and fairly penniless band. Their reason was that Charisma was the home of the prog-

rock band Genesis – who had once offered Taylor the drum position, which he declined – and that the label would inevitably prioritise the bigger band.

Instead, Testi spoke to Norman Sheffield, the owner of the renowned Trident Studios in Soho, who offered to manage Queen. This would enable the group to use the recording facilities while he searched for a record deal, and was an incredible opportunity for the band. This time, they grabbed it with both hands.

Queen now had a manager, a studio and a mission. Their task was now to take their message to the people.

CHAPTER 2
– The 1970s –

2

Don't

IF YOU SAW QUEEN IN THE
SEVENTIES, YOU WITNESSED A
ROCK PHENOMENON AT THE
ABSOLUTE PEAK OF ITS POWERS

WORDS *Joel McIver*

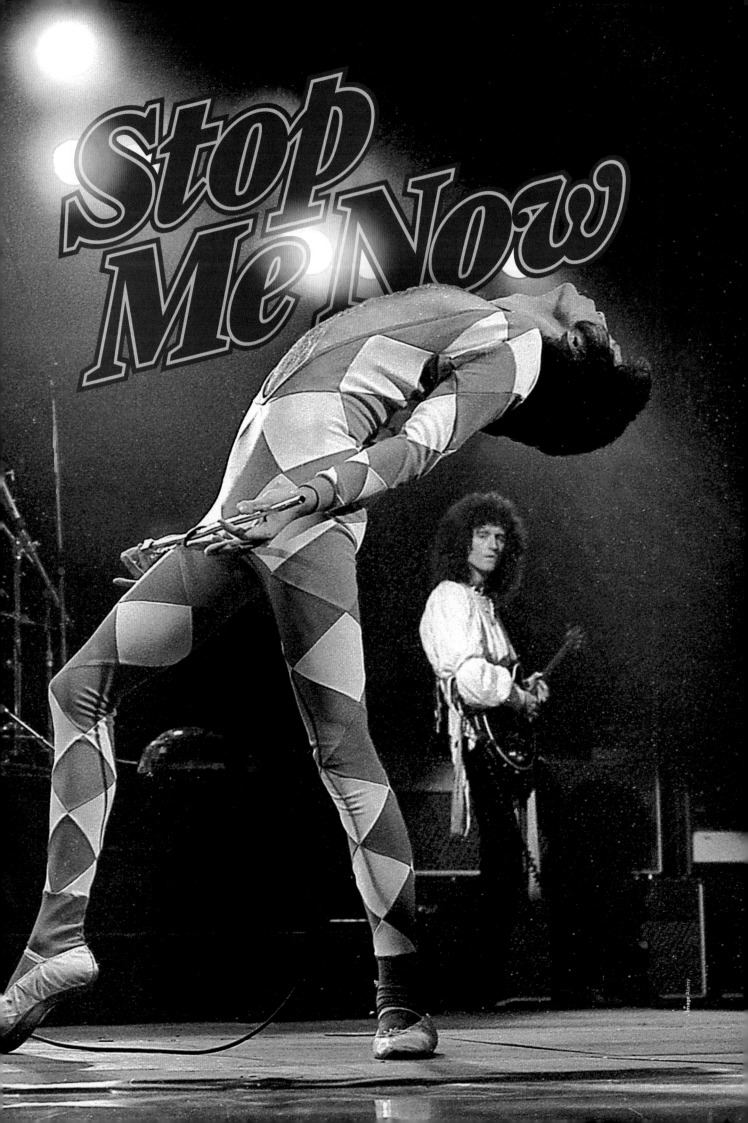

Stop Me Now

The Seventies was a decade of many aspects – outrageous fashions, experimental music and sociopolitical depression among them – but for Queen, it started not with a bang but with a whimper. It's hard to believe, given the size of their commercial impact later in the decade, that only six people came to see them play at Bedford College in London in early 1972. Then again, that reveals the speed and scale of Queen's upwards trajectory.

As with any far-reaching cultural phenomenon, time and effort was required before success came calling for Queen. Fortunately, huge inspiration was available in a performance by David Bowie and his backing band The Spiders from Mars, then touring Bowie's Ziggy Stardust incarnation. The single show attended by Queen on 29 January 1972 was a clear lesson to them that a powerful art direction means everything when it comes to music – at least when it's music of this level of ambition.

As Roger Taylor later recalled: "I got Freddie out in my little Mini... to Friars Aylesbury, which seemed like the end of the earth at that time. I think it could have been the first-ever Ziggy Stardust gig, and it blew us away – we were blown away. It was so fantastic, like nothing else that was happening and so far ahead of its time. The guy had so much talent to burn, really, and charisma to burn as well. I hate to gush, but he did have it like no one else did at the time."

In this light, Freddie's early on-stage persona makes perfect sense. A year older than Bowie, he would have realised with a start exactly how far ahead his contemporary was in confidence, panache and swagger, and stepped up his game accordingly. This is where Mr Mercury – the preening, don't-stop-me-now Mr Fahrenheit – was truly born: in a small club in a Buckinghamshire commuter town.

This epiphany came at just the right moment. Queen were tinkering with the songs on their self-titled debut album at Trident Studios, where they often

ABOVE Freddie during rehearsals for the band's first major tour in July 1973.

BELOW The band pictured in Copenhagen, Denmark during the Sheer Heart Attack Tour.

MIDDLE Performing 'Killer Queen' on *Top of the Pops* in November 1974.

of prestigious tours, including dates through 1973 in support of Mott The Hoople.

That said, the world wasn't quite ready to give Queen a free pass just yet. Their set at the Sunbury Pop Festival in Australia in January 1974 was received with mass derision by the audience. Glam-rock may have been dominating the charts at the time, but that doesn't mean that everybody liked the stuff, and Queen's operatic approach – and Freddie's sexually challenging persona – still caused some resentment outside centres of urban chic. In retaliation to the Sunbury crowd's mockery, Freddie declared: "When we come back to Australia, Queen will be the biggest band in the world!" His prophecy was

> 66 **Queen's music covered so much territory that it was impossible for them to please all the people all of the time** 99

disagreed with their producers John Anthony and Roy Thomas Baker on the direction and the mix of the tracks. The story goes that Brian May was keen to make the songs technically perfect, while everyone else preferred a more 'live in the studio' feel – and no one really had the experience to pull either objective off. Baker is known to have disliked the final album's "kitchen sink overproduction", as he called it, and the disagreements went so far that a song, 'Mad the Swine' was jettisoned from the track-listing because no one was willing to compromise on its sound.

Still, the *Queen* LP was complete by early '72, although the tapes sat around for some time before anyone heard them outside the industry. As any creative knows, making art is easy compared to persuading people to pay for it, and it took most of the year to secure a deal. A showcase gig took place at the Pheasantry venue on 6 November

followed by a gig at the Marquee Club on 20 December and EMI Records stepped up with a deal offer in March 1973.

This led to the release four months later of Queen's debut single, 'Keep Yourself Alive', and the album itself. Reviews were generally positive, with *Rolling Stone* labelling the *Queen* LP as "superb" – although that *RS* critic was either very perceptive or just in a good mood that day, because the album is far from Queen at their very best. 'Keep Yourself Alive' is a high point, but otherwise – as you can read in detail, elsewhere in this publication – it's the sound of a band finding its feet.

Still, Queen were now up and running, and sessions for *Queen II* followed immediately after the release of the debut LP. This time, studio time was more readily available and the musicians now had some expertise when it came to recording, and their rising profile led to a series

more or less accurate, although it took a couple more tours Down Under before Queen completely won the Aussies over.

1974 was the first Great Year of Queen, with the second album released in March and the single 'Seven Seas of Rhye' giving the group their first Top 10 hit. Reviews were mixed, but then they often were with Queen albums: critics tended to like the short rock hits but not the epic, extended prog workouts, or they liked the heavy songs but not the piano ballads, or the opposite, or any combination of the above. Even at this early stage, Queen's music covered so much territory that it was impossible for them to please all the people all of the time.

Not that the musicians themselves really cared. They had bigger things on their minds, not least their expanding theatrical image – Freddie, in particular, had become a clothes designer's dream – and the third →

album, the highly acclaimed *Sheer Heart Attack*. Half completed by the time May started work on it, as he'd been sidelined by a bout of hepatitis, the LP distilled all of Queen's strengths, hitting Number 2 in the UK and earning a gold award in the USA.

The songs 'Now I'm Here', 'Brighton Rock' and 'In the Lap of the Gods' were among those that showcased the range of the group, but the all-time standouts from the record are undoubtedly the excellent heavy metal romp 'Stone Cold Crazy' (later covered by Metallica) and the state-of-the-art 'Killer Queen', which reached Number 2 in the UK and 12 in the USA.

By the mid-point of the decade, Queen were bona fide stars, dominating their home country with every move they made and gaining a powerful foothold in America, always

the target of any aspiring global band. Thousands of fans swarmed to see them on their spring 1975 tour of the USA, despite some cancelled dates due to Freddie developing laryngitis, and the phenomenon soon continued into Japan, where they played eight shows in seven cities.

However, all was not well behind the scenes, in business terms at least. As was occasionally the case in such far-off times, the rewards which Queen were getting for their immense success were relatively paltry, with all four

members living in modest bedsits: Deacon was even refused a loan from Queen's managers, Trident, when he wished to buy a house. A split with Trident came in short order and new management was secured with Elton John's manager, John Reid, after Queen turned down an offer from Led Zeppelin's manager Peter Grant.

This turned out to be the best strategic move possible, because it enabled Queen to embark on their most ambitious recording project yet – their fourth album *A Night at*

the Opera, which borrowed its name from a Marx Brothers film of 1935. You can read more about this milestone LP elsewhere in this publication, but suffice it to say that it was a project – and a success – of genuinely huge dimensions.

While finely crafted songs such as 'Death on Two Legs', 'Lazing on a Sunday Afternoon' and 'The Prophet's Song' reached into new and astonishing musical territory, *A Night at the Opera* will, much like its creators, be most fondly and frequently remembered for 'Bohemian Rhapsody', a song that didn't so much occupy the intellectual rock medium as redefine it permanently. Released on Halloween 1975, a fact that has eluded many devoted Queen fans despite its theatrically thrilling nature, the song was only issued after a protracted fight with EMI, who thought it was too long. The accompanying video, a marvel of Seventies vision and technology, remains the default image associated with Queen for many of their followers.

ABOVE Relaxing in the garden of their Tokyo hotel while on tour in Japan, April 1975.

BELOW Queen invested a great deal in the production value of their shows.

> ❝ **By the mid-point of the decade, Queen were bona fide stars** ❞

'Bohemian Rhapsody' stayed at Number 1 in the UK for nine weeks, and is the third-best-selling single of all time in the country, beaten only by Band Aid's 'Do They Know It's Christmas?' and Elton John's 'Candle in the Wind 1997' – which makes it the biggest-selling non-charity song of all time. It was reissued in 1992 after Freddie's death, and in doing so became the only single ever to sell a million copies on two separate occasions, as well as becoming the Christmas Number 1 twice. Space doesn't permit a full listing of the subsequent charts and polls of various kinds that 'Bohemian →

Images Getty Images

> ❝ 'Bohemian Rhapsody' didn't so much occupy the intellectual rock medium as redefine it permanently ❞

Rhapsody' has conquered: let's just say that the only rock song of the entire Seventies that matches its cultural presence, even 50 years after the fact, is Led Zeppelin's 'Stairway to Heaven'.

You could reasonably argue that there were two phases in Queen's Mercury-era career: the five years before 'Bohemian Rhapsody' and the 16 years that remained to Freddie after it. That's how important it was to their trajectory. Songs of this magnitude often become something of a burden to the musicians who write them, and indeed the writing of the next album, *A Day at the Races* – also a Marx Brothers movie title – must have been influenced by its success.

Still, no one was complaining, as *A Night at the Opera* went triple platinum in the USA, boosted by its second single 'You're My Best Friend', and Queen's late-1975 Europe, North America, Japan and Australia dates, which cemented their presence in those territories yet again. A Christmas Eve concert at London's Hammersmith Odeon was broadcast on the BBC's *The Old Grey Whistle Test* and Radio 1, and was bootlegged for years before being officially released in 2015.

A Day at the Races was essentially a sequel to *A Night at the Opera*, from its artwork and title to the ambition of its songwriting. Although it didn't

have its own 'Bohemian Rhapsody' – with Queen wisely not attempting to replicate that particular behemoth – it came with a raft of career-best songs such as 'Somebody to Love', featuring the gospel-indebted vocal layers of Freddie, May and Taylor. May also supplied the riff-heavy 'Tie Your Mother Down', a song from the old-school heavy metal canon.

You couldn't escape Queen at this point in the late Seventies, even if you'd wanted to do so. They were in demand everywhere, it seemed, with the media permanently inquisitive about the musicians' private lives – that of Freddie in particular – and the band now playing at the highest level. On 18 September 1976 they played a

FAR LEFT Queen in rehearsals for the News of the World Tour at London's Shepperton Studios, October 1977.

ABOVE The band pictured during the shoot for the 'You're My Best Friend' music video, June 1976.

RIGHT John didn't sing on records, but occasionally sang backing vocals live.

BOTTOM RIGHT Roger speaking with Phil Lynott during the US leg of the A Day at the Races Tour in 1977, where Thin Lizzy were the opening act.

free concert in Hyde Park, organised by Virgin Records' Richard Branson, which broke attendance records when over 150,000 people turned up to see them. Times were different back then, and because the band went on late – and Freddie threatened to break the venue's curfew by returning to the stage for an encore – the police told him that he would be arrested if he did so. The establishment hadn't quite got the message yet, it seemed, that Queen were not like other bands.

Despite their huge and many successes, a wind of change was being felt in popular music, with a new and abrasive form of music – punk rock – making itself heard in late '76. On 1 December, Queen pulled out of the early-evening *Today* TV show, hosted by Bill Grundy, at the last minute: their replacement was a new group called the Sex Pistols. Intoxicated, irritated

and goaded by the hostile Grundy, the Pistols laid into him with a stream of swearing that made them infamous overnight, such was the power of light-entertainment television back then.

The bigger effect of the Pistols' tirade on the Grundy show was that bands such as Queen looked tame and irrelevant in comparison. Punk was loud, and so were Queen, but the difference was that bands like the Pistols were confrontational, obnoxious and working-class, making them a much more compelling spectacle than the intellectual Chopin and Zeppelin-worshipping fancies of Freddie et al.

The two factions – older rockers and newer punks – managed to rub along together most of the time, although there is a fabulous anecdote about the time when Freddie met the Sex Pistols' latter-day bassist John →

Ritchie, better known to the public as Sid Vicious. When the two men found themselves working in Wessex Studios in London on the same day in 1977, Vicious drunkenly said to the Queen singer, "Have you succeeded in bringing ballet to the masses yet?" in reference to a statement Freddie had recently made in the press.

Freddie's response was impressive: he simply drawled "Aren't you Simon Ferocious or something?" and – depending on which source you consult – either pushed him, threatened to hit him or simply had someone throw the inebriated Sex Pistol out. As Freddie himself explained: "He didn't like it at all. I said 'What are you going to do about it?' [...] He hated the fact that I could even speak [to him] like that. I think we survived that test."

Queen's mission continued despite such minor incidents, and the group executed the A Day at the Races Tour in 1977. These included sold-out shows at

Madison Square Garden in New York, where the support act was the Irish heavy rock band Thin Lizzy, whose singer Phil Lynott got on famously with Freddie and Taylor. Shows at Earls Court in London followed in June, with Queen celebrating the Silver Jubilee of Queen Elizabeth II with a lighting rig in the shape of a crown, said to have cost them £50,000.

The news of punk rock's arrival must have escaped the hundreds of thousands of people who lined up to buy Queen's sixth album, *News of the World*, on its release in 1977. Now a quadruple-platinum LP in the USA,

the album capitalised on the group's stadium-sized presence in that country by including two songs designed to motivate large crowds – 'We Will Rock You' and 'We Are the Champions'. Queen staged a truly huge production for the show that accompanied the new album, selling out shows worldwide.

Now, you could – if you wished – posit 1977 as Queen's creative peak. They had decades of enormous success ahead of them, as we know, but the flow of first-class albums effectively ended with the following year's *Jazz*, which was patchy despite its excellent singles 'Fat Bottomed Girls', 'Bicycle

> 66 **Huge tours proved that this merry foursome could still pull in a vast crowd at the click of a finger** 99

ABOVE In just a few years, Queen became one of the biggest bands of the decade.

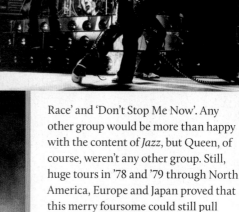

Race' and 'Don't Stop Me Now'. Any other group would be more than happy with the content of *Jazz*, but Queen, of course, weren't any other group. Still, huge tours in '78 and '79 through North America, Europe and Japan proved that this merry foursome could still pull in a vast crowd at the click of a finger, proven once again by the popularity of the in-concert album *Live Killers*, which was released in 1979 and quickly went double platinum.

Queen wound up this incredible decade with a single, 'Crazy Little Thing Called Love', which surprised fans in two ways – its rock'n'roll style and the fact that Freddie played guitar on it, both in the studio and on stage. The song was a triumph, becoming Queen's first Number 1 in the United States, and staying at the top of the charts in Australia for seven consecutive weeks.

The decade ended on a high when, on 26 December 1979, Queen were asked by Paul McCartney – one of the very few bigger names in British rock music than Freddie and his band – to play the opening night at the Concert for the People of Kampuchea in London.

You think *you* had a good time in the Seventies? Now think what that decade must have been like for Freddie, Brian, John and Roger... 👑

Images Getty Images, Alamy

When we began,
we approached it the
way we did because
we were not prepared
to be out-of-work
musicians, ever.
We said either take
it on as a serious
commodity or don't
do it at all.

Freddie Mercury in an interview
with *Melody Maker*, May 1981

QUEEN

UK RELEASE DATE **JULY 1973**
HIGHEST CHART POSITION **24**
KEY TRACK **KEEP YOURSELF ALIVE**

A glorious hard rock marathon unlike anything else around at the time, this album started it all. In fact, any other band might have given up, such were the unpromising circumstances that greeted Queen's arrival onto the London scene in the early 70s.

There was Brian, the nerdy space brain who'd built his own guitar from a fireplace (a what?); John Deacon, another bright boy, who always looked the most doubtful; or as he said: "I knew there was something," but wasn't "convinced of it"

until long after Queen became stars; Roger Taylor, the pretty, blond ex-public schoolboy from Cornwall who'd studied to become a dentist; and up front the brilliant Farrokh Bulsara – Freddie to his friends – who'd come from a boys' boarding school in India and was an arty, fashion-freaked, Hendrix-obsessed, pan-sexual dynamo who'd renamed himself Mercury after a line in one of his own songs. ("Mother Mercury, look what they've done to me," from this album's 'My Fairy King'.)

Tracklist

1 Keep Yourself Alive
2 Doing All Right
3 Great King Rat
4 My Fairy King
5 Liar
6 The Night Comes Down
7 Modern Times Rock 'n' Roll
8 Son and Daughter
9 Jesus
10 Seven Seas of Rhye (Instrumental)

> 66 **This may have been Queen taking baby steps, but the sound of their future is all here** 99

Maybe it was the unmistakably unique sound of Brian May's home-made guitar. Perhaps it was the panoramic production of Roy Thomas Baker, or the soaring voice of Freddie Mercury. Whatever the secret, *Queen* was one of those scary albums that simply burst its seams. The record was just too powerful, too multi-dimensional and too stunning to sit happily and contentedly in the grooves. The performances were all virtuoso. And those songs... oh, those songs: beginning with the cast-iron 'Keep Yourself Alive', breathless and languid

in the same phrase, then 'Great King Rat', 'Son & Daughter' while 'Liar', the album's second single, served as a superbly dramatic vehicle for Queen's harmony vocals, May's guitar and the band's ability to tell stories with their music, the album finishing with a brief, early instrumental version of 'Seven Seas of Rhye'. This may have been Queen taking baby steps, but the sound of their future is all here: silks, satins, elaborate feathercuts, Zeppelin-esque riffs and Beach Boys harmonies. This was the stuff of legend. ♕

QUEEN II

UK RELEASE DATE **MARCH 1974**
HIGHEST CHART POSITION **5**
KEY TRACK **SEVEN SEAS OF RHYE**

FROM THE
ROCK
ARCHIVE
2014

"For a long time it was my favourite Queen album," Brian May told *Classic Rock*. "It got overtaken by *Made in Heaven*, but I've always loved that record. In a sense it was the biggest jump we ever made creatively."

Queen II is arguably the heaviest Queen album. They had pushed their rock and metal roots as far as they could, and were clearly looking to jump off the train and expand their horizons. 'Ogre Battle' hit the metal trail, 'The March of the Black Queen' offered prog-rock

retribution, 'Father to Son' was eerily catchy and 'Nevermore' was a prime-cut ballad.

In its bombastically glorious sound, its sonic grandeur, its sometimes hilarious excesses, *Queen II* is the record that pointed the way to the band that they would become. From a cover shot in homage to Marlene Dietrich, to its themed sides of White and Black, unfettered ambition runs through it. Forty five years later, it retains a gobsmacking appeal.

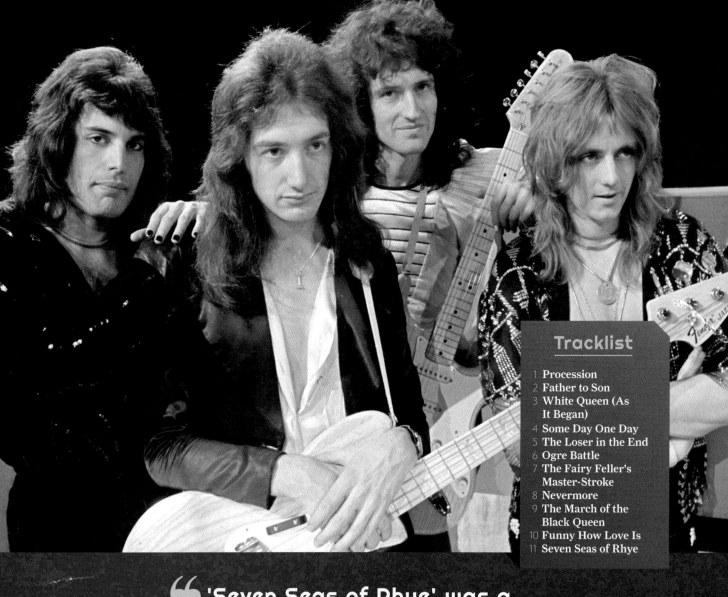

Tracklist

1 Procession
2 Father to Son
3 White Queen (As It Began)
4 Some Day One Day
5 The Loser in the End
6 Ogre Battle
7 The Fairy Feller's Master-Stroke
8 Nevermore
9 The March of the Black Queen
10 Funny How Love Is
11 Seven Seas of Rhye

> ❝ 'Seven Seas of Rhye' was a pocket epic that referenced both Greek mythology and British seaside humour ❞

"I remember *Queen II* clearly because it was such a formative period," said Roger Taylor. "*Queen II* was more of a piece, rather than just being songs thrown onto an album, which is what the first one was. We were really starting to push the boundaries of the studio in terms of overdubbing, and what we could do vocally."

Queen II also marked Queen out as a band who could write hit singles. Their first attempt, 'Keep Yourself Alive', had flopped the previous year. This time there would be

no mistake. Tucked away at the end of the album, 'Seven Seas of Rhye' was a pocket epic that referenced both Greek mythology and British seaside humour. Crucially, the band wrote it specifically to be a hit. "Everything including the kitchen sink got thrown at that," explained May. "'Pressure' isn't the right term, it was more: we would like to have our single played on the radio, so let's not give them any excuse not to." 'Seven Seas of Rhye' peaked at No.10 in the UK chart – the first in an astonishing run of 54 Top 40 singles. ♔

Words: Jon Hotten Images: Getty Images

SHEER HEART ATTACK

UK RELEASE DATE **NOVEMBER 1974**
HIGHEST CHART POSITION **2**
KEY TRACK **KILLER QUEEN**

FROM THE
ROCK
CLASSIC
ARCHIVE
2011

Unlike *Queen* and *Queen II*, *Sheer Heart Attack* was conceived in the studio, albeit through necessity rather than by design. "Nobody knew we were going to be told we had two weeks to write *Sheer Heart Attack*," explained Mercury. "And we had to – it was the only thing we could do. Brian was in hospital." (The guitarist had been diagnosed with hepatitis.)

Despite the setbacks, there was no doubt among the band that *Sheer Heart Attack* would take them to the next level. The black-and-white approach of *Queen II* had been reigned in and replaced by a kaleidoscopic range of sounds and styles. Leading this new approach was 'Killer Queen', an outrageously camp ditty that was closer to Noël Coward than to Robert Plant.

"That was the one song which was really out of the format that I usually write in," said Mercury. "Usually the music comes first, but the words, and the sophisticated style that I wanted to put across in the song, came first."

Tracklist

1 Brighton Rock
2 Killer Queen
3 Tenement Funster
4 Flick of the Wrist
5 Lily of the Valley
6 Now I'm Here
7 In the Lap of the Gods
8 Stone Cold Crazy
9 Dear Friends
10 Misfire
11 Bring Back That Leroy Brown
12 She Makes Me (Stormtrooper in Stilettos)
13 In the Lap of the Gods... Revisited

> ❝ The black-and-white of *Queen II* had been replaced by a kaleidoscopic range of sounds and styles ❞

If 'Killer Queen' was the best-known song, it was hardly representative of the album, largely because the band didn't chain themselves to one style. No band other than The Beatles had dared throw as many different styles into the mix with as much confidence. That state of affairs in Queen was helped by the fact that all four members pitched in with the writing.

A convalescing May delivered the rockers, including 'Now I'm Here' and opener 'Brighton Rock'. Bookended by a picaresque tale of two seaside lovers sung in high and low registers by Mercury, it was a showcase for an extended May guitar solo. By contrast, Mercury threw in everything from waspish glam rock ('Flick of the Wrist', a reflection of their increasingly strained relationship with their management) to old-fashioned vaudeville ('Bring Back That Leroy Brown', complete with ukulele solo from May). Most prescient was 'In The Lap of the Gods', a two-part, near-operatic epic that laid the groundwork for 'Bohemian Rhapsody' the following year. Clearly Queen were on the verge of something spectacular... ♛

A NIGHT AT THE OPERA

UK RELEASE DATE DECEMBER 1975
HIGHEST CHART POSITION 1
KEY TRACK BOHEMIAN RHAPSODY

FROM THE
CLASSIC
ROCK
ARCHIVE
2017

Yes, the one with 'Bohemian Rhapsody', the most played and analysed rock anthem ever. *A Night at the Opera* was the record where Queen really delivered in terms of diversity. You want metal? There's 'Death on Two Legs' and 'Sweet Lady'. Pop? 'I'm In Love with My Car' and 'You're My Best Friend'. Camp ditties? 'Seaside Rendezvous' and 'Lazing on a Sunday Afternoon'. Even a proggie moment: '39'. Finishing with 'God Save the Queen' was a moment when pretension, ego and self-deprecation collided perfectly.

Over-familiarity, *Wayne's World* and over-exposure might have taken the shine off 'Bohemian Rhapsody'. Yet its release, its daring fusion of heavy metal, show-tune balladry and light opera remains the high-water mark on *A Night at the Opera*, and a tribute to 70s Queen's collective imagination and sheer bravado. It broke the mould in 1975, and no-one has even dared to try and compete with it since.

One song does not an *Opera* make, however, and there's more to the album than 'Bohemian Rhapsody'. There's John

Tracklist

1	Death on Two Legs (Dedicated to...)	6	Sweet Lady
2	Lazing on a Sunday Afternoon	7	Seaside Rendezvous
3	I'm in Love with My Car	8	The Prophet's Song
4	You're My Best Friend	9	Love of My Life
5	39	10	Good Company
		11	Bohemian Rhapsody
		12	God Save the Queen (Instrumental)

Deacon's 'You're My Best Friend', a lush pop song that sounds like T. Rex remodelled by The Beach Boys, and was Deacon's first hit single, reaching the UK's top 10. Freddie brought 'Love of My Life', a romantic ballad (reputedly written for Mercury's soon-to-be- ex-girlfriend Mary Austin) that became an audience singalong at shows in the late 70s. Roger Taylor had a love song too – except his was about his car. 'I'm In

apart from being close to its best, is certainly its most vicious. Lyrics such as "You suck my blood like a leech" were aimed at Queen's ex-co-manager Norman Sheffield, and were so vituperative the now late Sheffield threatened Queen with a lawsuit. From its Hammer Horror movie intro through May's scything guitar solo and Mercury's impassioned "You're tearing me a-p-a-r-t", this is Queen at their rococo rock finest.

> ❝ 'Bohemian Rhapsody''s fusion of heavy metal and light opera remains the album's high-water mark ❞

Love with My Car' was the B-side to 'Bohemian Rhapsody' and vintage Taylor. With his blond girl's hair and fine line in self-aggrandising, laddish rock songs (see also: 'Tenement Funster'), 'I'm In Love with My Car' captures the essence of Queen's barefaced cheek and grandeur. Plus, any song that rhymes "forget her" with "carburettor" can't be all bad, can it?

So there's love songs, there's charm and wit – but there's vitriol too. Freddie Mercury could be a vicious sod, and 'Death on Two Legs', the opening track on *A Night at the Opera*,

And we've almost gone all this way without mentioning Brian May. His '39' – a song he once described as "sci-fi skiffle" – has a sing-song campfire melody and simple charm that make it his best song on the album. Not that he was slacking. Most guitarists would have been happy to put their feet up after coming up with the various riffs, solos and licks on 'Rhapsody'. Instead May is on fine form, establishing the gorgeous melodic style that would become his signature. Team work makes the dream work. ♜

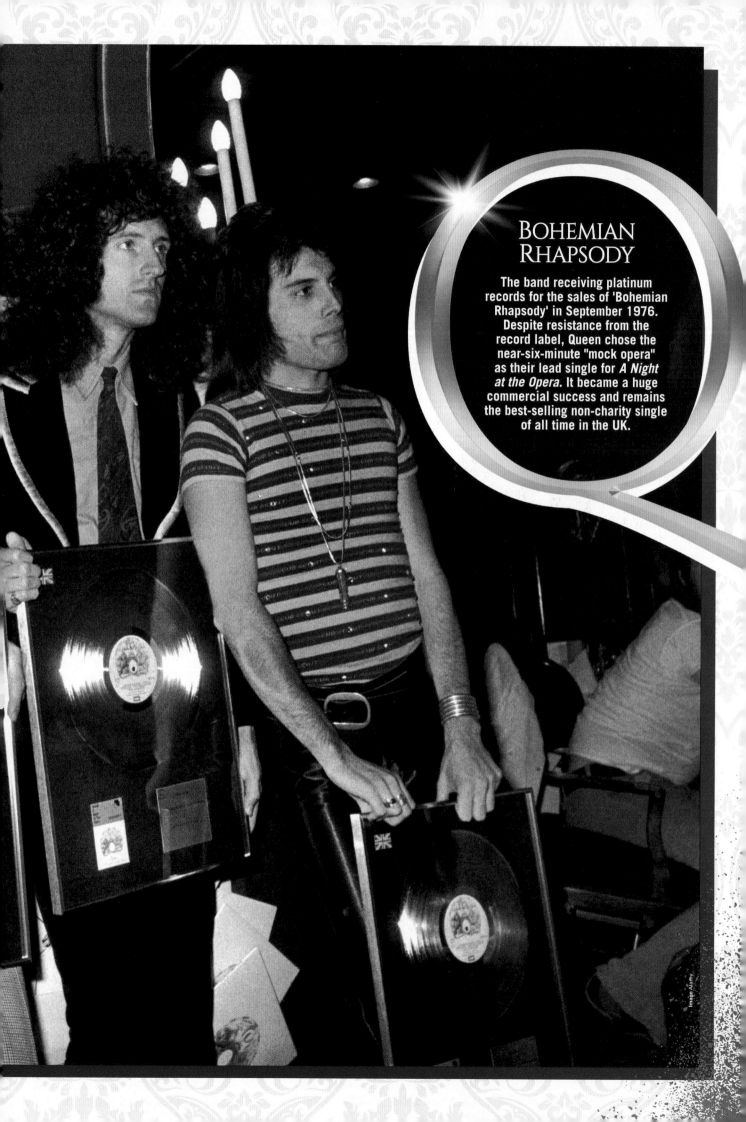

BOHEMIAN RHAPSODY

The band receiving platinum records for the sales of 'Bohemian Rhapsody' in September 1976. Despite resistance from the record label, Queen chose the near-six-minute "mock opera" as their lead single for *A Night at the Opera*. It became a huge commercial success and remains the best-selling non-charity single of all time in the UK.

A DAY AT THE RACES

UK RELEASE DATE **DECEMBER 1976**
HIGHEST CHART POSITION **1**
KEY TRACK **SOMEBODY TO LOVE**

Many bands who had achieved even ten per cent of what Queen had with *A Night at the Opera* would have sat back on their laurels. But not Queen. Back in the studio, the band were determined to find the right balance between wanting to follow up *...Opera* and doing something completely new.

A Day at the Races concentrated on pushing musical boundaries while keeping the focus firmly on mainstream messaging. The album's two longest tracks barely broke five minutes: there was Mercury's gloriously effete 'You Take My Breath Away' and May's winsome 'Teo Torriatte (Let Us Cling Together)', the latter of which was written as a thank you to the band's dedicated Japanese fanbase.

There was 'Tie Your Mother Down'. Brian May had written the hooky guitar riff years before. Then there was the pop-rock apotheosis 'Good Old-Fashioned Lover Boy', making the most of its pure Queen vocal harmonies and tippity-top use of ragtime jazz.

Tracklist

1 Tie Your Mother Down
2 You Take My Breath Away
3 Long Away
4 The Millionaire Waltz
5 You and I
6 Somebody to Love
7 White Man
8 Good Old-Fashioned Lover Boy
9 Drowse
10 Teo Torriatte (Let Us Cling Together)

> ❝ 'Somebody to Love' became characterised as this album's 'Bohemian Rhapsody' ❞

And of course there was rock with a capital 'R'. The days of white queens and fairy kings may have been long gone for Queen, but that didn't prevent Brian May from bringing out the lead when it suited him. The lyrics to 'White Man' may be cringe-inducing to modern ears, but those mountainous guitars and drums, though, they do not lie.

The album's finest moment, by far – and one of the most transcendent moments in the history of rock – was 'Somebody to Love'. At the time, it became characterised as this album's 'Bohemian Rhapsody'. That is, the pivotal track, with its multi-layered harmony vocals and butterflying Mozartian piano being the very essence of what had most intrigued the world about 'Bo Rhap'.

Yet it was different in so many ways. Those extravagant vocals, for example, weren't conceived from opera, but from gospel. As John Deacon later explained, 'Somebody to Love' proved that "Queen could swing as hard as it could rock, by channelling the spirit of gospel music". ♕

Words Mick Wall Images Getty Images

NEWS OF THE WORLD

UK RELEASE DATE NOVEMBER 1977
HIGHEST CHART POSITION 4
KEY TRACK WE WILL ROCK YOU

FROM THE
ROCK
ARCHIVE
2017

Yes, the album's got 'We Are the Champions' and 'We Will Rock You', two songs so embedded into the social fabric it's easy to forget their origins. So it's also easy to see *News of the World* as being about these tracks and nothing else. But that does the album a massive disservice. Although Queen were loath to admit it, the thinking behind *News...* had in fact been more than a little influenced by the lacklustre reception *A Day at the Races* had received – and not just from the critics. Designed very much as what their former producer Roy Thomas Baker decried as a record that "absolutely screamed 'sequel'", it had sold less than a third of what *A Night at the Opera* had sold in both Britain and America, and less than half what it had sold worldwide. Not a flop, but not "the way things should be going", as Roger Taylor put it.

Whatever they did next, it became abundantly clear to everyone in Queen that the follow-up to *...Races* would have to be a little different. The buzz word around the new album was 'spontaneity'.

Roger Taylor brought in demos of two tracks. The first, 'Sheer Heart Attack', was originally aborted from the sessions for the album of the same name and redirected as Taylor's 'answer' to punk. Punchy, repetitive, two- chord fury: "Well you're just 17 and all you wanna do is disappear / You know what I mean there's a lot of space between your ears..." The second, 'Fight from the Inside', was essentially more of the same, with Taylor on lead vocals, and again having a not-so-sly dig at the punks who saw the 28-year-old idol as now somehow past it. "You're just another picture on a teenage wall, you're just another sucker ready for a fall..."

It was the band's principal songwriters, Mercury and May, who came up with the most potent ripostes to any claim

bugling guitar solo, was the first real rock anthem to gain traction since the heyday of what we now think of as classic rock. Populist, all-inclusive, this was the 'come on in, the water's fine' rock anthem at its most affecting. It was a song for the people to sing along to; to clap their hands and stamp their feet to.

The 'We' in 'We Are the Champions' was again meant as a you and me, in it together, banner call, but with some more subtle, reflective intentions. "I can understand some people saying 'We Are the Champions' was bombastic," admitted May some years later. "But it wasn't saying Queen are the champions, it was saying all of us are. It made the concert like a football match, but with everyone on the same side."

 It was Mercury and May who came up with the most potent ripostes to any claim that Queen had lost their mojo 99

that Queen had lost their mojo, with two of the finest, most memorable and long-lasting tracks of their career: May's 'We Will Rock You' and Mercury's 'We Are the Champions'.

A delicious coincidence, perhaps, but the fact that both tracks used the pronoun 'we' said a great deal about how the band saw themselves in terms of their own loyal fanbase, and the slings and arrows they had suffered on their behalf. 'We Will Rock You', with its captivating 'boom-boom-tush' rhythm and whiplash vocals, topped off by that marvellously

May did the real heavy lifting in terms of songwriting, contributing four tracks, including 'We Will Rock You', two of which, 'All Dead, All Dead' and 'Sleeping on the Sidewalk', he also sang lead vocals on – the first time it really hit home just how close May's voice was to Mercury's. May's other contribution was made of much more substantial stuff: the six-minute 'It's Late' was one of the album's major highlights.

News of the World continued Queen's strong run of albums, while proving they weren't prepared to stand still.

Words Mick Wall Images Getty Images

JAZZ

UK RELEASE DATE **NOVEMBER 1978**
HIGHEST CHART POSITION **2**
KEY TRACK **DON'T STOP ME NOW**

FROM THE **CLASSIC** **ROCK** ARCHIVE **2019**

It's often criticised for being a little too off-the-wall and idiosyncratic for general consumption, yet listen closely and *Jazz* offers some of the most satisfying moments in Queen's career. Titled more for the fact that May, Mercury, Deacon and Taylor now felt they could go anywhere musically than for the style of the songs, *Jazz* took some extreme turns.

'Mustapha' had a Middle-Eastern sense of humour, 'Fat-Bottom Girls' was a cod-macho piss-take and 'Bicycle Race' offered up some neat *Carry On* film-inspired double entendres (Queen decamped to Switzerland to work on the album and the song's inspiration came from the '78 Tour de France passing through Montreux, the location of Mountain Studios). 'Don't Stop Me Now' was the Broadway song Cole Porter never wrote, 'Fun It' had disco pretensions, and 'Dreamers Ball' came straight at us from the music-hall stage.

Jazz wasn't a true rock album, but its spirit reflects the fact that nobody understood better than Queen what rock music could achieve. ♔

Images Getty Images

Tracklist

66 Listen closely and *Jazz* offers some of the most satisfying moments in Queen's career 99

CHAPTER 3
– The 1980s –

It's a Kind of Magic

WHILE THEIR RIVALS STUMBLED,
QUEEN HIT THE '80S LIKE A TRAIN.
FROM DRUGS AND DISCOS TO
CLASHES WITH DAVID BOWIE,
THIS IS THE STORY OF THE BRITISH
BAND'S IMPERIOUS DECADE

WORDS *Henry Yates*

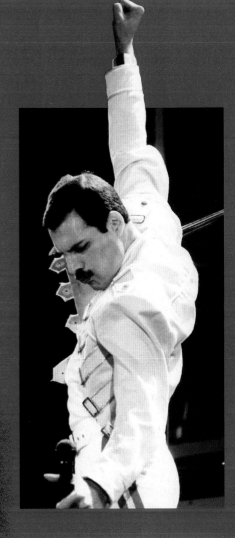

I t was 1980, and the giants of rock'n'roll were dropping like flies. By the year's end, Led Zeppelin drummer John Bonham's doomed drinking session would also drag his band to the grave. While the surviving members of a Moon-less Who scattered to solo careers, The Rolling Stones and Pink Floyd stagnated, toiling over half-forgotten records whose filler songs would rarely trouble their stadium setlists.

Amidst this cull of rock dinosaurs, Queen were champing at the bit for a second imperious decade. Having signed off the '70s with their biggest

Stateside single so far – the boot-clicking rockabilly homage of 'Crazy Little Thing Called Love', composed by Freddie Mercury in the bubbles of a Munich bathtub – by February 1980, the band were ready to go again. With producer Reinhold Mack, the four members hunkered at the Bavarian city's Musicland Studios, where a four-month writing streak birthed 40-plus songs for the longlist of that year's *The Game*.

In Munich, Brian May was the night owl, often to be found at the Musicland mixing desk "at three o'clock, trying to make something work". When they ventured out, the guitarist and his rhythm section could be found testing new material over the speakers of

> 66 Even when fist-tight as a creative unit, Queen's chemistry could still be combustible 99

ABOVE RIGHT While other '70s artists struggled, Queen became one of the defining bands of the '80s.

ABOVE Queen's 'Under Pressure' collaboration with David Bowie came about while they were all recording at Mountain Studios in Montreux, Switzerland.

RIGHT The group pose for a photoshoot in Tokyo, February 1981.

downtown discotheque Sugar Shack. "We would take tracks down there after hours and play them over their system to see how they worked," recalled May. "Anything with a bit of groove and space sounded good. We became obsessed

with leaving space in our music and making songs that would sound great in the Sugar Shack."

The club was referenced lyrically on May's funky 'Dragon Attack' ("Take me to the room where the black's all white and the white's all black", sings Mercury over hot-buttered bass. "Take me back to the Shack"). But the thumbprint of Munich's nightlife was perhaps most overt on the band's biggest hit of the decade, which also spliced John Deacon's formative love of Motown and the osmosis of Chic's 1979 album *Risqué* (which he had heard Bernard Edwards recording in New York).

Played on a single low string, the spare three-note bassline of 'Another One Bites the Dust' didn't sound like much – May has said "[we] had no idea what Deacy was doing". But when the band fell in, the combined groove was irresistible, with Taylor's clipped beats meeting May's uncharacteristic chicken-scratch funk chords and Mercury reportedly singing "until his throat bled". →

Images Getty Images

ABOVE The band performing in Leiden, The Netherlands, during The Game Tour in November 1980.

But even when fist-tight as a creative unit, Queen's chemistry could still be combustible. Perhaps May still didn't entirely trust Mack: the producer had previously told the guitarist to trade his beloved Red Special for a snappier-sounding Fender Telecaster on 'Crazy Little Thing Called Love', and now the pair disagreed on *The Game*'s guitar tracking approach. Nursing solo aspirations (his own debut, *Fun in Space*, would follow in April 1981), Taylor seemed more interested in his Oberheim OB-X synth than his drumkit and pushed his way to the mic for 'Rock It'. As Mack told iZotope: "Keeping the focus was difficult at the best of times with this mixture of personalities."

Mercury's take was less diplomatic. *The Game* sessions, he once said, were "four cocks fighting". And while Taylor reflected that the band was "functioning well", he conceded "there were huge rows in the studio. Usually over how long Brian was taking, or whether he was having an omelette. We drove each other nuts."

"We all walked out at various times," noted May. "You get hard times, as in any relationship. We definitely did. Usually in the studio; never on tour. On tour, you always have a clear, common aim. But in the studio you're all pulling in different directions and it can be very frustrating. You only get twenty-five per cent of your own way at the best of times. So, yes, we did have hard times. Feeling that you're not being represented, that you're not being heard. Because that's one of the things about being a musician, you want to be heard. You want your ideas to be out there. You want to be able to explore what's coming to you in the way of inspiration. It was a difficult compromise to find, but always worth finding once you did find it."

Whether their status was war or peace, at least Queen were still bankable. Released in June 1980, *The Game* topped both the US and UK charts, its leather-jacketed sleeve shot announcing a sartorial rebirth as these '70s dandies crossed over into a new epoch. And while a 46-date US tour was crowned by a show at Madison Square Garden, a bolder move was trekking to South America the following year, to satisfy the demands of a continent whose radios throbbed with Deacon's bassline.

Trailed by an armed convoy between Buenos Aires, Mar Del Plata, Rosario and São Paulo – and guarded, shuddered Mercury, by "the heavy police who actually kill people at the drop of a hat" – Queen would gross $3.5 million and start a love affair with the South American nations that endures to this day. "The government, actually, wanted us to be here," reflected the singer of what was then a trailblazing visit. "I think they wanted The Rolling Stones or us or whatever. A lot of the groups were scared to come here in the early days, as it were. And we took the plunge."

> **Mercury and Bowie jostled for control of the 'Under Pressure' vocal during a 24-hour session at Montreux's Mountain Studios**

ABOVE LEFT The Game Tour saw Queen perform in South America for the first time.

FAR LEFT Freddie and Roger on stage in Oakland, California, in 1982.

LEFT The Hot Space Tour included 69 dates across Europe, North America and Japan.

That summer, the second of Queen's undeniable '80s hits was born from an altogether frostier atmosphere, as Mercury and David Bowie jostled for control of the 'Under Pressure' vocal during a 24-hour session at Montreux's Mountain Studios. "It was very hard," recalled May of the wine and cocaine-fuelled marathon, "because you already had four precocious boys and David, who was precocious enough for all of us. Passions ran very high. I found it very hard because I got so little of my own way. But David had a real vision and he took over the song lyrically."

As Queen's latest UK#1 single, 'Under Pressure' seemed to signpost a band in imperious form. But that march would be disastrously broken by May 1982's *Hot Space* album: a spanner dropped in the Queen machinery due to what Taylor called a "fairly decadent" lifestyle and the divisive presence of Mercury's personal manager Paul Prenter, said by one associate to "lead Freddie by the nose".

Despite his guitar work being virtually wiped off the mix, May was defiant ("I make no apologies for the *Hot Space* album – it got us out of a rut and into a new place"). Yet the wider reaction suggested he was a lone voice. Following *The Game* out onto the disco dancefloor, but with diminishing returns, this tenth album was every bit as bloodless as ice-funk lead single 'Body Language', shipped in a sleeve that Taylor deemed "absolute shit", stalled at US#22 and

was drowned out by jeers when the band performed its offcuts live. "If you don't want to listen to it then fucking go home," snapped Mercury when 'Staying Power' failed to live up to its name onstage in Germany.

The *Hot Space* lyrics – mostly celebrating Mercury's nights on the prowl – even stuck in the band's craw. "I can remember having a go at Freddie because some of the stuff he was writing was very definitely on the gay side," →

Images Getty Images

57

said May. "I remember saying it would be nice if this stuff could be universally applicable, because we have friends of every persuasion."

Trading these divisive wares, the band schlepped across North America, but when the curtain fell at the LA Forum – as it turned out, the final US date the original lineup ever played – May admitted that "we hated each other for a while".

While their ire cooled, solo work scratched an itch without bothering the charts. May and Eddie Van Halen's *Star Fleet Project* proved a cult concern outside axe-hero circles, while Mercury bounced between side-hustles both underwhelming (1985's work-in-progress *Mr Bad Guy*) and abortive (a session with Michael Jackson that never was). But with the mothership calling, by August 1983, the lineup fell in at the Record Plant in Los Angeles, where Taylor fired back at criticism of his recent output with the undeniable 'Radio Ga Ga': a

juddering electro-ballad at once wistful and triumphant that would be chalked onto Queen setlists forevermore. "I think Roger was thinking about it as just another track," said Mercury, who finished off the song. "But I instantly felt there was something in there, a really good, strong, saleable commodity."

Elsewhere, the new sessions threw it all at the wall. May struck uncomplicated rock-god poses on the crunching 'Hammer to Fall'. Deacon quietly supplied another classic with the yearning 'I Want to Break Free', while Mercury was elegant and empathetic on 'It's a Hard Life' (and ridiculous in the prawn suit he wore for the video). "I think we look more stupid in that video," sighed Taylor on the commentary for the *Greatest Video Hits 2* DVD, "than anyone has looked in a video ever."

But what to call this cornucopia of sound and vision? *The Works*, suggested Taylor, and the title stuck. Where the empty futurism of *Hot Space* had burnt

off swathes of the band's '70s fanbase, this eleventh album won them back with a sound that felt ambitious but rooted in that formative classic-rock sound. "I see it as being a lot closer to the middle period than the last three or four albums," May told *Guitar World* as the album marched to UK#2 and stuck in the chart for 93 weeks. "It's a lot closer to *A Night at the Opera* and *News of the World* and a little bit like *The Game*. But some of the writing is the next step beyond, it's not going back in time. Because we've integrated some of the modern technologies. But we haven't gone totally towards machine music because the fact is we don't like it."

The only sticking point was America, its vast tracts of Bible Belt enraged by the 'I Want to Break Free' video, which found Mercury dragged up as a desperate housewife in a bra and leather miniskirt, vacuuming the house. "I know it was received with horror in the greater part of America," May told Mick

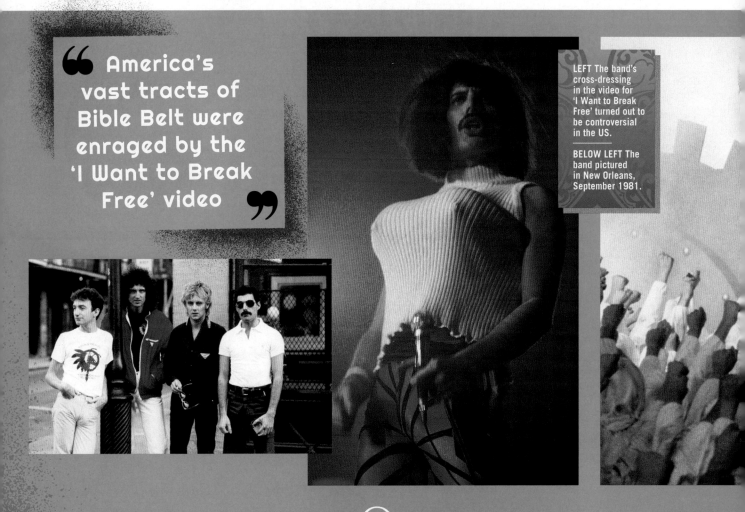

> " America's vast tracts of Bible Belt were enraged by the 'I Want to Break Free' video "

LEFT The band's cross-dressing in the video for 'I Want to Break Free' turned out to be controversial in the US.

BELOW LEFT The band pictured in New Orleans, September 1981.

Wall. "To them it was boys dressing up as girls and it was unthinkable, especially for a rock band. I was actually in some of those TV stations when they got the thing and a lot of them refused to play it. They were visibly embarrassed about having to deal with it. And we were not seen for quite a long time in the States. Freddie didn't want to go back smaller than we'd been before. He was like: 'Let's just wait, and then soon we'll go out and we'll do stadiums in America as well.' Only of course we never did."

If their penchant for cross-dressing hobbled Queen's success in the States, then the band's international ambitions almost wiped them off the board entirely. In the early-'80s, South Africa still operated a hateful policy of racial segregation, and while a glance at the Sun City holiday resort developed by hotelier Sol Kerzner suggested paradise, the azure swimming pools and verdant gardens belied its billing as the 'apartheid Las Vegas', ring-fenced as a no-go zone for musicians in the United Nations' cultural boycott.

BELOW Queen's last performance in the US before Freddie's death was on *Saturday Night Live* in September 1982.

BOTTOM The video for 'Radio Ga Ga' was directed by David Mallett and featured clips from *Metropolis* (1927).

By playing a residency at Sun City in October 1984, Queen were following a run of marquee names including Rod Stewart and Elton John. Moreover, the band's moral stance made perfect sense, with May stressing that shows were watched by an integrated audience. "Those criticisms are absolutely and definitely not justified," he told *Smash Hits*. "We're totally against apartheid and all it stands for, but I feel that by going there, we did a lot of bridge building. →

Images Getty Images, Alamy

BELOW Brian, Roger, Freddie and John at the Golden Rose Festival in Montreux, Switzerland in May 1986.

We actually met musicians of both colours. They all welcomed us with open arms. The only criticism we got was from outside South Africa."

Upon their return, a fine from the Musicians' Union was a mere bee sting for a band of Queen's stature. What hurt more was their portrayal as a band on the wrong side of history, at a time when Steven Van Zandt's Artists United Against Apartheid were railing at South African policy – 'I ain't gonna play Sun City!' ran the key lyric in the 1985 protest song named after the resort – and *NME* cover stars like Paul Weller condemned all those who broke the red line.

Vilified and wounded, Queen found redemption the only way they knew how: with a run of impossibly epic shows that reminded fans of music's unique capacity to heal and unite. Performing to over half a million South American fans in January 1985, Rock in Rio could hardly be described as a warm-up. Yet it would take Bob

Geldof's invitation to that summer's Live Aid to fully rehabilitate Queen in the eyes of both the 72,000 fans within Wembley Stadium and the 2 billion more watching around the world. Not bad, considering that May told *Smash Hits* the band had almost ducked the occasion. "Our first reaction was 'Oh God! Not another one'. We'd been involved in quite a few and we were a bit disillusioned as to how the whole business works."

If the UK#1 placing of June 1986's *A Kind of Magic* album suggested fortunes restored, the uptick was confirmed by the 26-date Magic Tour that played to over 400,000 fans at flagship venues including Slane Castle, Wembley Stadium and Knebworth Park, while grossing more than £11 million. Just as important, after the disastrous hands-across-the-water gesture in South Africa, was July's stop at the Népstadion in Budapest, which restored Queen's socio-political credentials as woke

ABOVE Freddie and John pictured during the band's visit to Budapest, Hungary, in 1986.

BELOW LEFT Freddie in Tokyo, September 1986, while he and partner Jim Hutton were holidaying in Japan.

> ❝ It would take Bob Geldof's invitation to that summer's Live Aid to fully rehabilitate Queen in the public eye ❞

rock musicians, rousing 80,000 souls in a country then tightly controlled by Communist strongman prime minister György Lázár. As Mercury broke from the Queen catalogue to sing the Hungarian traditional 'Tavaszi Szél Vizet Áraszt' – referring to the lyrics jotted on his hand – the "fucking deafening" response remembered by May seemed like the icing on a perfect night.

But perhaps that victory in Budapest offered the first hint of something darker, too. The enquiry from the local Hungarian reporter was innocent enough: did the singer intend to return

to Eastern Europe someday? In the summer of 1986, Mercury was still a year away from officially receiving the HIV diagnosis that would kill him in November 1991, aged 45. Though he would quit the stage after Knebworth, for now the singer remained a vital force as a performer and had a brace of albums left in him, with 1989's *The Miracle* subsequently reaching UK#1 with some of the band's most ambitious songs since the '70s.

And yet, already, there were whispers that the end of the road was close. You saw the gathering storm clouds in the ghoulish tabloid splashes about Mercury's 'secret illness'; in the claims of those close to the singer that they had seen him display symptoms; and in the deaths of those closer still (including former boyfriend Tony Bastin, who passed away at Christmas 1986).

So, would Mercury return to Budapest? The singer paused for a beat before giving a reply that was pure gallows humour: "If I'm still alive..." ♛

"I have to win people over, otherwise it's not a successful gig. It's my job to make sure people have a good time. That's part of my duty.

Freddie Mercury in an interview with *The Sun*, 1985

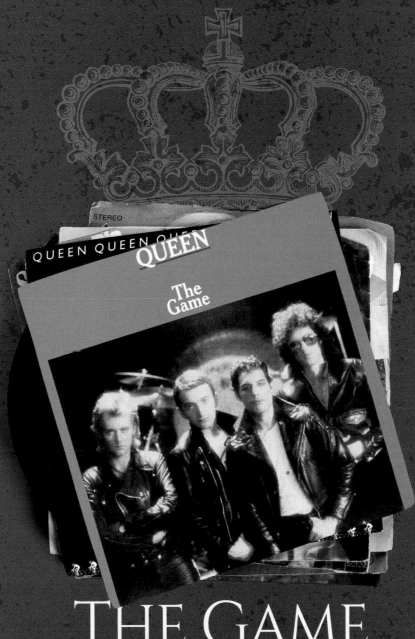

THE GAME

UK RELEASE DATE **JUNE 1980**
HIGHEST CHART POSITION **1**
KEY TRACK **ANOTHER ONE BITES THE DUST**

Working with German engineer Mack gave Queen the opportunity to expand their sound – most notably breaking their own 'No Synthesisers' edict. *The Game* featured the band's two biggest US singles, the rock'n'roll throwback 'Crazy Little Thing Called Love' and the unfeasibly funky 'Another One Bites the Dust', as well as the soaring ballad 'Save Me'. But the deeper cuts were far from fillers. Vicious live favourite 'Dragon Attack' and 'Rock It (Prime Jive)' are among the most underrated of all Queen tracks.

The rockabilly pastiche 'Crazy Little Thing Called Love' was dreamt up by Freddie Mercury in a Munich bathtub and captured at that city's Musicland Studios, the single seemed the launchpad to an imperious decade – even if Brian May told *Guitar World* that the lineup operated less through design than dumb luck: "Everyone thought we had this huge monster plan, the Queen Machine, but it's an illusion."

Happy accident or otherwise, by February 1980, the band were keen to capitalise, returning to the same Bavarian studio

Tracklist

1 Play the Game
2 Dragon Attack
3 Another One Bites
  the Dust
4 Need Your Loving
  Tonight
5 Crazy Little Thing
  Called Love
6 Rock It (Prime Jive)
7 Don't Try Suicide
8 Sail Away Sweet Sister
9 Coming Soon
10 Save Me

> **The rockabilly pastiche 'Crazy Little Thing Called Love' gave the quartet their biggest US hit**

for a four-month hot-streak, where the four members' prolific output was underlined by the 40-odd songs pitched for inclusion on that year's record.

John Deacon's inspired bassline for 'Another One Bites the Dust' was the product of both his Motown-fixated youth and a chance overhearing of US funk icons Chic's 1979 album *Risqué*. And while the rest of the band were bemused – May recalling that "The rest of us had no idea what Deacy was doing when he started [the track]" and that Taylor's initial response was "This isn't rock'n'roll, what the hell are we doing?" – they soon fell into the groove. According to May, Mercury "had a feel for dance music, and he was starting to fall in love with singing that way. He was so into what we were doing with 'Another One Bites the Dust' that he sang until his throat bled".

"For me, the band was functioning well at this point," noted Taylor. "*The Game* was much more of a piece than *Jazz*. Our songwriting was much better." ♛

Words Henry Yates Images Getty Images

FLASH GORDON

UK RELEASE DATE DECEMBER 1980
HIGHEST CHART POSITION 10
KEY TRACK FLASH'S THEME

This was the soundtrack to the uproariously camp film of the same title, and given the nature of the movie itself, Queen were the perfect band to come up with the music. They did a fine job, but without the visuals much of the music's impact is lost. In fact, it's almost entirely instrumental, which is what you'd expect for a soundtrack. Only 'Flash's Theme' and 'The Hero' had lyrics. The former is the most well known song here, and perfectly sums up the serious yet spoof nature of the film.

The thumping 'Flash's Theme' is one of the great Queen singles (and features some prime dialogue from the film, not least Brian Blessed's iconic, immortal battle cry of "Gordon's alive!"), while 'The Hero' isn't far behind.

Like the characters on screen, *Flash Gordon* as an album was hilarious, because it was done with a completely straight face. The rest of the album has a tongue-in-cheek grandeur that fits the film, but without the visuals much of the music's impact is lost. It's far from awful, it's just inessential. ♔

Tracklist

1 Flash's Theme
2 In the Space Capsule (The Love Theme)
3 Ming's Theme (In the Court of Ming the Merciless)
4 The Ring (Hypnotic Seduction of Dale)
5 Football Fight
6 In the Death Cell (Love Theme Reprise)
7 Execution of Flash
8 The Kiss (Aura Resurrects Flash)
9 Arboria (Planet of the Tree Men)
10 Escape from the Swamp
11 Flash to the Rescue
12 Vultan's Theme (Attack of the Hawk Men)
13 Battle Theme
14 The Wedding March (based on "Bridal Chorus")
15 Marriage of Dale and Ming (And Flash Approaching)
16 Crash Dive on Mingo City
17 Flash's Theme Reprise (Victory Celebrations)
18 The Hero

66 *Flash Gordon* as an album was hilarious, because it was done with a completely straight face 99

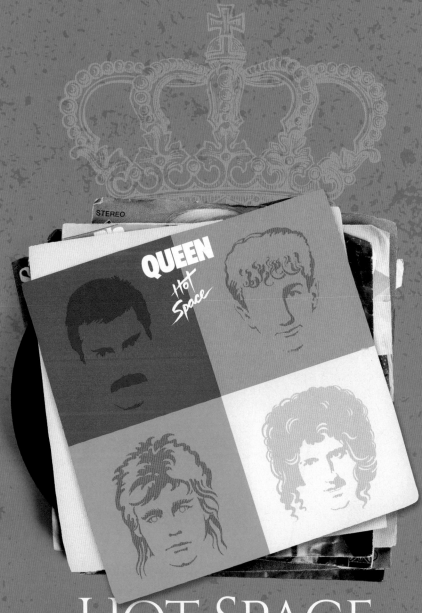

HOT SPACE

UK RELEASE DATE **MAY 1982**
HIGHEST CHART POSITION **4**
KEY TRACK **UNDER PRESSURE**

FROM THE
CLASSIC
ROCK
ARCHIVE
2018

Let's face it. There are no total duds in the Queen catalogue, just albums which might be comparatively disappointing. Of these, *Hot Space* is certainly one of the most culpable. It was Queen's slightly misguided attempt to break into the dance market, and while they had the musical chops to carry this off, the whole thing comes across as a patchwork, inconsistent record.

"I make no apologies for the *Hot Space* album," said Brian May. "I was well into it at the time. It took me a while to get into that philosophy of sparseness but it was very good for us, it was a good discipline and it got us out of a rut and into a new place."

The main problem isn't the style of the music, it's the songwriting. With the exception of the excellent 'Under Pressure' (a collaboration with David Bowie) and the engaging 'Body Language', a sleek, highly impressive electro-disco bump'n'grind, the rest of the album falls short of the standard Queen fans took for granted. 'Under Pressure' is an

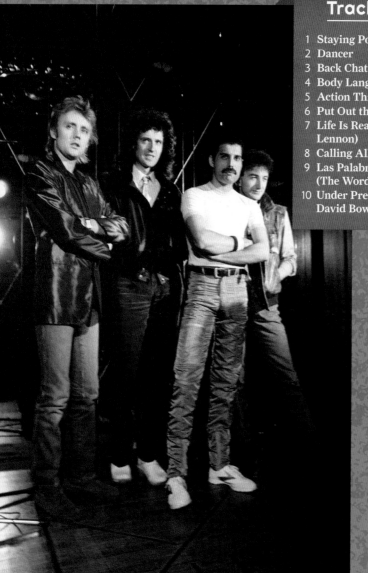

Tracklist

1 Staying Power
2 Dancer
3 Back Chat
4 Body Language
5 Action This Day
6 Put Out the Fire
7 Life Is Real (Song for Lennon)
8 Calling All Girls
9 Las Palabras de Amor (The Words of Love)
10 Under Pressure (with David Bowie)

> ❝ *Hot Space* was Queen's slightly misguided attempt to break into the dance market ❞

absolute banger, though, and Roger Taylor is right to call this song "one of the very best things Queen have done".

The first time Queen collaborated with another artist they got their second UK No.1. Both Queen and Bowie happened to be in Montreux and were at a BBQ at the home of promoter Claude Nobs. "I said to them: 'You don't always have Queen and David Bowie together so why don't you go into the studio and see what you can do?'" recalled Nobs. According to Mercury, the collaboration was "virtually a 24-hour session" and was fuelled by "a few bottles of wine and things".

The resulting track is underpinned by one of the finest basslines in pop history from John Deacon, but most of the arrangements were done by Mercury whose soaring vocals, while a perfect complement to Bowie's, steal the show quite spectacularly (including a mind-bending falsetto A5). Bowie apparently wanted to re-record it all, but Queen's sense of spontaneity prevailed. ⬤

Words Mick Wall. Images Getty Images

GREATEST HITS

The band collecting their gold discs for *Greatest Hits* in April 1982. To date, the compilation is the best-selling album of all time in the UK and has been certified an astonishing 23x platinum.

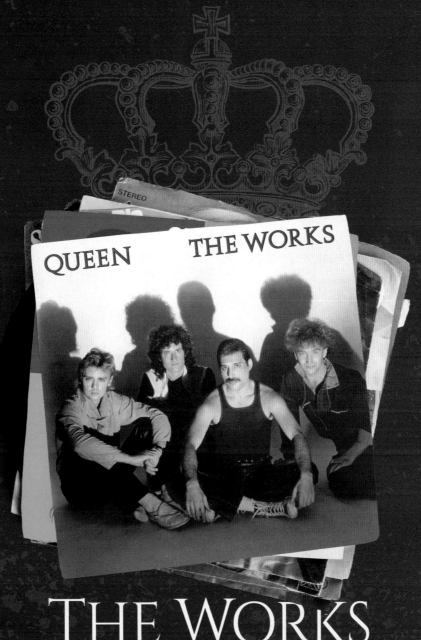

THE WORKS

UK RELEASE DATE **MARCH 1984**
HIGHEST CHART POSITION **2**
KEY TRACK **I WANT TO BREAK FREE**

FROM THE
CLASSIC
ROCK
ARCHIVE
2018

For the Queen traditionalists, the release of *The Works* in 1984 proved to be an unexpected joy. To call it a return to form would be unjust. It was another move forward, just less deliberately weird than its oft-derided predecessor. The electronics were there not just to unbalance expectations, but, as in royal days of yore, to become another Queen-endorsed part of the overall musical majesty. The album's title reportedly came from a comment Taylor made during production: "Let's give them the works!"

It is a satisfying album that worked the band's hard rock roots back into the equation without sacrificing the electropop and funk strata they'd been embracing over the previous few years. The alliance of these styles worked in a smooth manner. Perhaps taking a break after *Hot Space* had re-energised them all for the challenge of a new Queen album. Whatever the reasons, *The Works* pressed all the right buttons. 'Hammer to Fall' was a vibrant return to guitar-saturated power. 'Radio Ga Ga', written by Taylor, was a giant

Tracklist

1. Radio Ga Ga
2. Tear It Up
3. It's a Hard Life
4. Man on the Prowl
5. Machines (or 'Back to Humans')
6. I Want to Break Free
7. Keep Passing the Open Windows
8. Hammer to Fall
9. Is This the World We Created...?

> " It's a satisfying album that worked the band's hard rock roots back into the equation "

hit, heralding what appeared to be a new chapter in the ever-unfolding story of Queen.

Even better, though, was 'I Want to Break Free', with its gorgeous loping rhythm that John Deacon had again come up with, and blissfully muted synth solo, played by the great Fred Mandel, the first significant extracurricular musician ever to appear on a Queen record. The single's accompanying music video was a hoot, of course, with its cringingly short skirts, crooked women's wigs, badly drawn lippy and droopy cigarettes. The track was fabulous, joyous and, when listened to alone, away from the hoovering video, a wonderfully fully realised demand for the one thing rock music was originally invented to champion: the freedom to be oneself, whoever the hell that might be, when no one else is looking.

The record remains their longest-charting studio album in the UK, with a cumulative 94 weeks. With *The Works*, Queen had rediscovered their desire to be leaders of the pack. ♚

Words Mick Wall Images Getty Images; Avalon/Simon Fowler (main).

A KIND OF MAGIC

UK RELEASE DATE MAY 1986
HIGHEST CHART POSITION 1
KEY TRACK A KIND OF MAGIC

In some respects – like *Flash Gordon* before it – this was a soundtrack album. Six of the songs were included in *Highlander*, and while 'A Kind of Magic' was never written and recorded as a soundtrack album, it became one by default.

The style here swept across the rock spectrum, accentuating the band's strengths along the way. Wherever they trod, Queen still managed to be grandiose in the manner only they could achieve. Songs like 'A Kind of Magic', 'One Vision' and 'Who Wants to Live Forever' quickly became iconic, while the piano ballad 'Friends Will Be Friends' and the heavy 'Princes of the Universe' were hardly slouches.

'Princes of the Universe' has many of the glossy 80s movie soundtrack tropes you might expect, but with all the stomping, overtly theatrical Queen pomp you might not. The band knew how to deliver what a movie demanded, and this song – with its hard-edged metallic riffs and creeping sense of unease – is one of the heaviest they produced in the 80s. It was a glorious reminder that Queen still knew how to rock. Hard.

Tracklist

1 One Vision
2 A Kind of Magic
3 One Year of Love
4 Pain Is So Close
   to Pleasure
5 Friends Will
   Be Friends
6 Who Wants to Live
   Forever
7 Gimme the Prize
   (Kurgan's Theme)
8 Don't Lose Your Head
9 Princes of the
   Universe

 **In some respects –
like *Flash Gordon* before it
– *A Kind of Magic* was
a soundtrack album**

'One Vision' was the first single to be released with a "written by Queen" credit. Inspired by their epoch-defining Live Aid performance, the tune is built around a suitably girthsome guitar riff and fleshed out by yet another brilliant vocal performance. It demonstrates the band's ability to play within any style, and even though the song's construction is fairly obvious. The middle eight – composed of electronica and studio trickery – shows off the humour inherent throughout the band's output and often overlooked.

Oh, and your ears aren't deceiving you; the final lyric is indeed "fried chicken", motivated by the band's gnawing hunger after a long day in the studio and the result of some Mercury-led vamping during the recording process.

A sister to 'One Vision', 'A Kind of Magic' was another high-quality pop song written by Roger about his utopian vision of the world. Its title was inspired by a line from *Highlander* and moulded into a hook-laden pop masterpiece with the band's customary aplomb. ♛

Images Getty Images

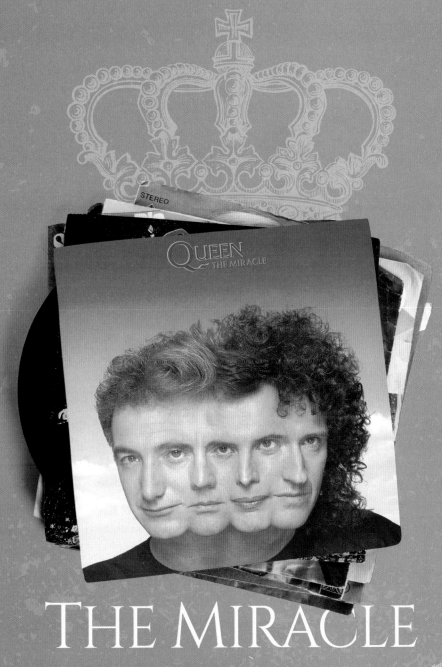

THE MIRACLE

UK RELEASE DATE MAY 1989
HIGHEST CHART POSITION 1
KEY TRACK I WANT IT ALL

FROM THE CLASSIC ROCK ARCHIVE 2019

Queen's 13th album, *The Miracle*, was released in May 1989 and capped a rollercoaster decade for the band – one that had swung from the highs of the monumental Stateside success of 'Another One Bites the Dust's to the lows of their much maligned disco and funk influenced 1982 album *Hot Space*, and back up again to the twin triumphs of the Live Aid and Knebworth mega-shows.

The latter had been Queen's live swansong, but that didn't stop *The Miracle* becoming yet another huge success for the band, hitting Number One in the UK and across Europe, and yielding five singles including 'I Want It All', 'Breakthru' and 'The Invisible Man'.

Yet there was darkness behind the scenes. Freddie Mercury had been diagnosed with AIDS before the band recorded *The Miracle*, although this remained a closely guarded secret within Queen's inner circle.

The Miracle was originally going to be called *The Invisible Men*, which would have hardly been appropriate for such

Tracklist

1 Party
2 Khashoggi's Ship
3 The Miracle
4 I Want It All
5 The Invisible Man
6 Breakthru
7 Rain Must Fall
8 Scandal
9 My Baby Does Me
10 Was It All Worth It

a high-profile band. This time around, the mix of musical styles ranged from the progressive title track to the pomp pop flow of 'I Want It All' and the electro funk of 'The Invisible Man' (which namechecked all four members in its lyrics). 'Breakthru', despite starting off with a delicate piano intro, soon gives way to a rollicking, upbeat rocker. Also, listen out for that Don Henley 'Boys of Summer'-inspired

some time, but not tabloid fodder until the last three years. It's not been pleasant. Some papers want a certain kind of news, and it can wreck people's lives."

In a departure from previous Queen releases, *The Miracle*'s songs were not credited to individual songwriters. "When we came to make this album, we made a decision that we should have made fifteen years ago," Brian May told *Sounds* upon its

> ❝ **The album is triumphant thanks to Mercury's stunning vocals and May's agitated guitar work** ❞

chord sequence. "I very much like this track," said May at the time. "It's a Roger track, full of energy."

'Scandal' was an especially noteworthy song, being written by May as an attack on the British media, who had hounded the guitarist over his developing relationship with actress Anita Dobson, and also for the way they treated Freddie Mercury as he privately battled AIDS.

"We've all been hauled through the tabloids now," May said. "It's very strange that we've been moderately famous for

release. "We decided that we'd write as Queen, that we would credit everything to the four of us, so that nobody would leave a song alone. It also helps when we choose singles, because it's difficult to be dispassionate about a song that's purely of your own making."

Although swathed in synth sounds, the album is triumphant thanks to Mercury's stunning vocals and May's agitated guitar work. The balance between all the styles worked out better than might have been feared. ✍

CHAPTER 4
– Queen Live –

Killer

NOBODY COULD TOUCH THE CLASSIC QUEEN LINEUP AS A LIVE FORCE. HERE ARE FIVE STANDOUT SHOWS THAT ROCKED US…

WORDS *Joel McIver*

Since their 1970 formation, the Rainbow Theatre had seemed beyond Queen's reach. The legendary 3,000-capacity venue in London's Finsbury Park was a stop-off for such giants as Jimi Hendrix, Eric Clapton, David Bowie and The Beach Boys – while Queen's most recent trek had been as support for glam-rockers Mott The Hoople.

But on 31 March 1974 – the same month *Queen II* was released – the band stepped up. "We'd done our support tour," recalled May in *The Greatest* video series. "Then promoter Mel Bush came to us – he was a pretty top promoter at the time – and said, 'I think you guys can headline the next tour'. We were surprised. I remember thinking 'Wow, that's very quick,' because normally you would support a few acts and build a following. He gave us a big list – Newcastle City Hall, Manchester's Free Trade Hall or whatever – all the classic gigs that rock bands do – and he said, 'You can fill all these and then, at the end, we're going to do the Rainbow.'"

The subsequent release of *Live at The Rainbow '74* (including the March show and their return that November) showcased a lineup firing on all cylinders, from the anthemic 'Seven Seas of Rhye' to the roof-raising 'Keep Yourself Alive', extended with a thunderclap Taylor drum solo. Queen had arrived. ♕

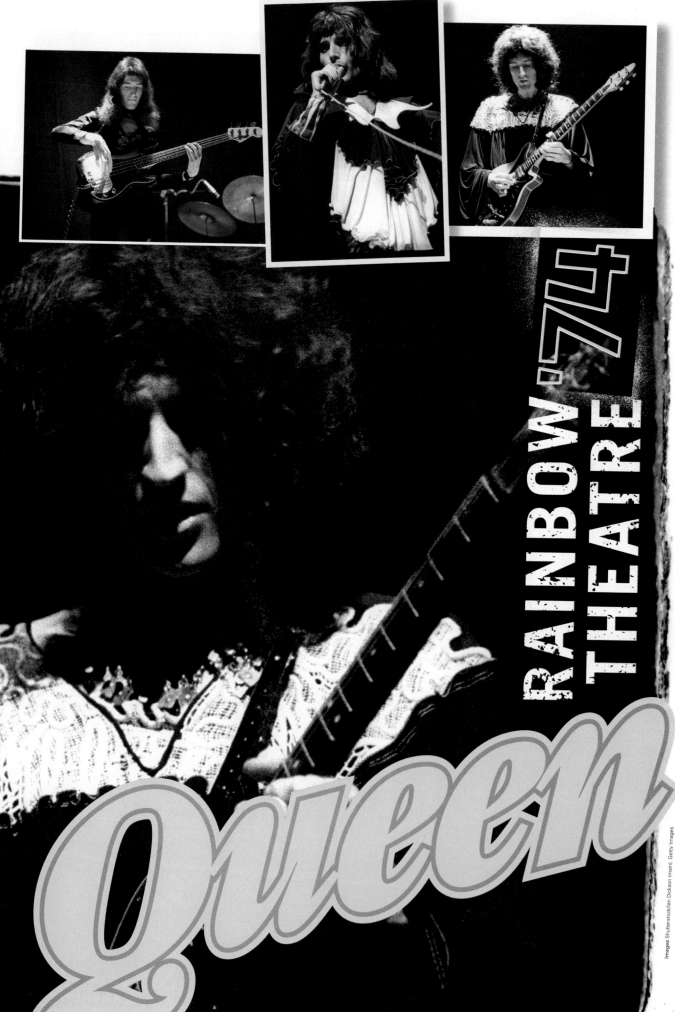

RAINBOW '74 THEATRE

Queen

ROCKIN IN RIO '85

If North America's love affair with Queen had cooled a little by the mid-'80s, the band's riotous two-night stand in Brazil proved the South still had a passion verging on mania. Now an annual institution, the Rock in Rio festival was taking its ambitious first steps in January 1985. Everything about the inaugural event was on an epic scale, from the purpose-built 250,000m² Cidade do Rock venue to the sprawling ten-day lineup studded with legends including AC/DC, Rod Stewart, Iron Maiden and Yes. The most staggering statistic of all was the attendance, pegged at almost 1.5 million.

Surveying that roiling human sea, even Freddie Mercury seemed uncharacteristically edgy, admitting his "first-night jitters" to an interviewer who caught him before Queen's performance. But when the band took the stage at 2am, the old magic reignited in a set that served up the hits and mined 1984's multi-platinum album, *The Works*, to seismic effect. And if there was a worrying moment when Mercury was pelted with detritus while performing a drag act for 'I Want to Break Free', he made amends by flipping a double-sided Union Jack flag to reveal the Bandeira Do Brasil.

When the dust settled, the statistics were hard to compute, with Queen having played for up to 300,000 paying audience members each night – a record at the time – while each of their televised performances was watched by an estimated 200 million viewers. No stranger to grandiosity, even Mercury was lost for words: "It's mind-boggling…" ♛

LIVE AID
'85

Twenty minutes. That's how long it took for Queen to stake their claim as the era's greatest rock band and bury their rivals on the Live Aid bill. The 1985 charity concert was, quite simply, the biggest stage on Earth. Armed with the moral leverage of the Ethiopia famine, and dangling the kind of global exposure that no rock'n'roll ego could refuse, organiser Bob Geldof's press-gang campaign had been brutally effective, lining up old guardsmen like The Who and Paul McCartney alongside rising forces like U2 and Dire Straits.

By contrast, Queen were navigating a slippery career patch, losing ground in the US and criticised for a controversial run at South Africa's Sun City. Recognising Live Aid as their shot at redemption, the band took time to prepare, cherry-picking from their catalogue and honing their six chosen songs to a razor's edge. 'Bohemian Rhapsody' was hacked from its six-minute studio length but still ran the emotional gamut. The hard-rocking 'Hammer to Fall' butted against the wistful 'Radio Ga Ga', offset by playful rockabilly pastiche 'Crazy Little Thing Called Love', the deathless stompalong of 'We Will Rock You' and arms-aloft finale, 'We Are the Champions'.

That hot afternoon in July 1985, the reaction of the 72,000-strong Wembley Stadium crowd, and the 2 billion more watching across the planet, said it all. Queen stole the show, the day, the whole damn era. Backstage, Elton John told *The Guardian* in 2019, he had approached Mercury to congratulate him. "And Freddie said, 'You're absolutely right, darling, we killed them…'"

By July 1986, Queen were no strangers to Wembley Stadium: it was on this same hallowed stage that the band had been reborn the summer before at Live Aid. But to sell out the fabled national stadium under their own banner, remembered Brian May in one video interview, was sweeter still. "Wembley is special because it's your hometown and it's a legend [...] Live Aid was a terrific blast, but to come back and play it ourselves and sell it out [was amazing]."

Roger Taylor had not been shy in his promotional soundbites ahead of Queen's twin performances on July 11th and 12th ("It will make *Ben Hur* look like *The Muppets*," promised the drummer). Sure enough, for the 72,000 ticket-holders who flooded into Wembley each day for this stop-off on the Magic Tour, the razzmatazz was without precedent, from the twin ego ramps that let Freddie Mercury meet his public to the iconic fur-trim crown and gown the singer had commissioned from designer friend Diana Moseley.

Backstage, there was anxiety ("The first moment when you hit the guitar, the first point of the show is always a terrific rush," reflected May, "and you do feel nervous"). But the band needn't have fretted. Heavily rehearsed and opening the set with recent single 'One Vision', this was Queen at the dizzy peak of their live powers, hitting all the vital songs from their catalogue and shooting down whispers they were almost at the end of the road. "We're going to stay together," Mercury promised the crowd, "until we fucking well die..." 👑

'86

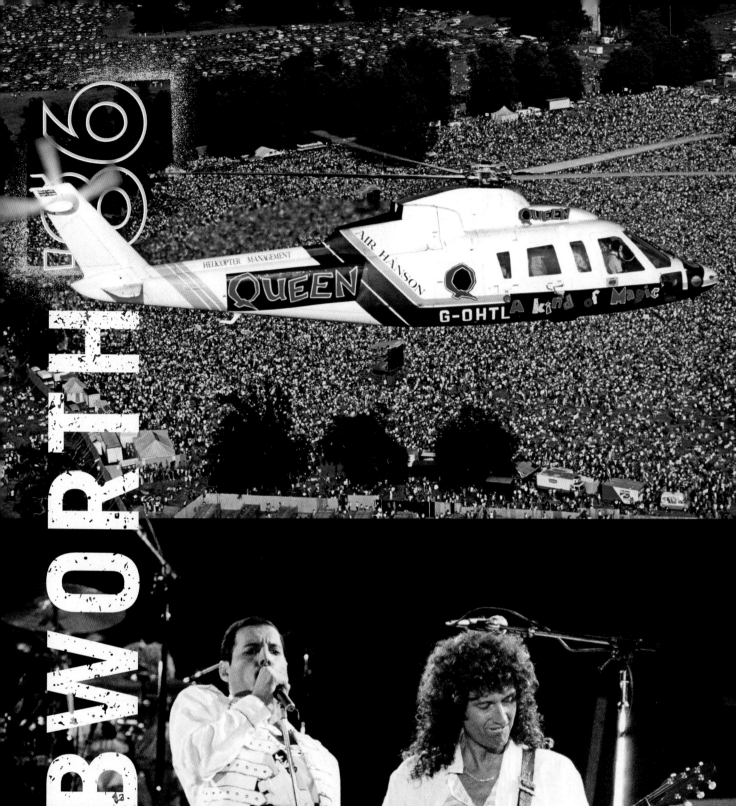

KNEBWORTH 86

With appetite for the Magic Tour proving insatiable, promoter Harvey Goldsmith added the mother of all finales at the Hertfordshire country estate where only rock's true galacticos could sell out. Even then, he remembered, the booking lines were jammed. "We have a capacity at Knebworth Park of 120,000, and on the first day of tickets going on sale, we sold 30,000 tickets. They seem to have an endless market."

By the day of the concert on 9 August, it was already whispered in the tabloids that Freddie Mercury had visited Harley Street for an AIDS test, but you would never have guessed at the storm clouds to come from the singer's formidable last stand at Knebworth. With the band touching down in a custom-painted helicopter, the original lineup played as if they knew the end was nigh, tearing through a career-spanning set that began with 'One Vision' before alighting on 'I Want to Break Free', 'Crazy Little Thing Called Love', 'We Will Rock You' and 'Radio Ga Ga' (after which the usually sweet-natured John Deacon smashed his bass against his amp).

"Goodnight and sweet dreams," announced Mercury at the end of encore 'God Save the Queen', before dropping the bombshell to his bandmates backstage that Queen would henceforth be a studio-only operation. "We had done the biggest tour ever of our lives and it was a great success and we were very happy," recalled Brian May in the documentary *The Final Act*. "And then Freddie said, 'I can't do this anymore…'"

CHAPTER 5
– The 1990s –

IS THIS THE REAL LIFE? IS THIS JUST FANTASY?

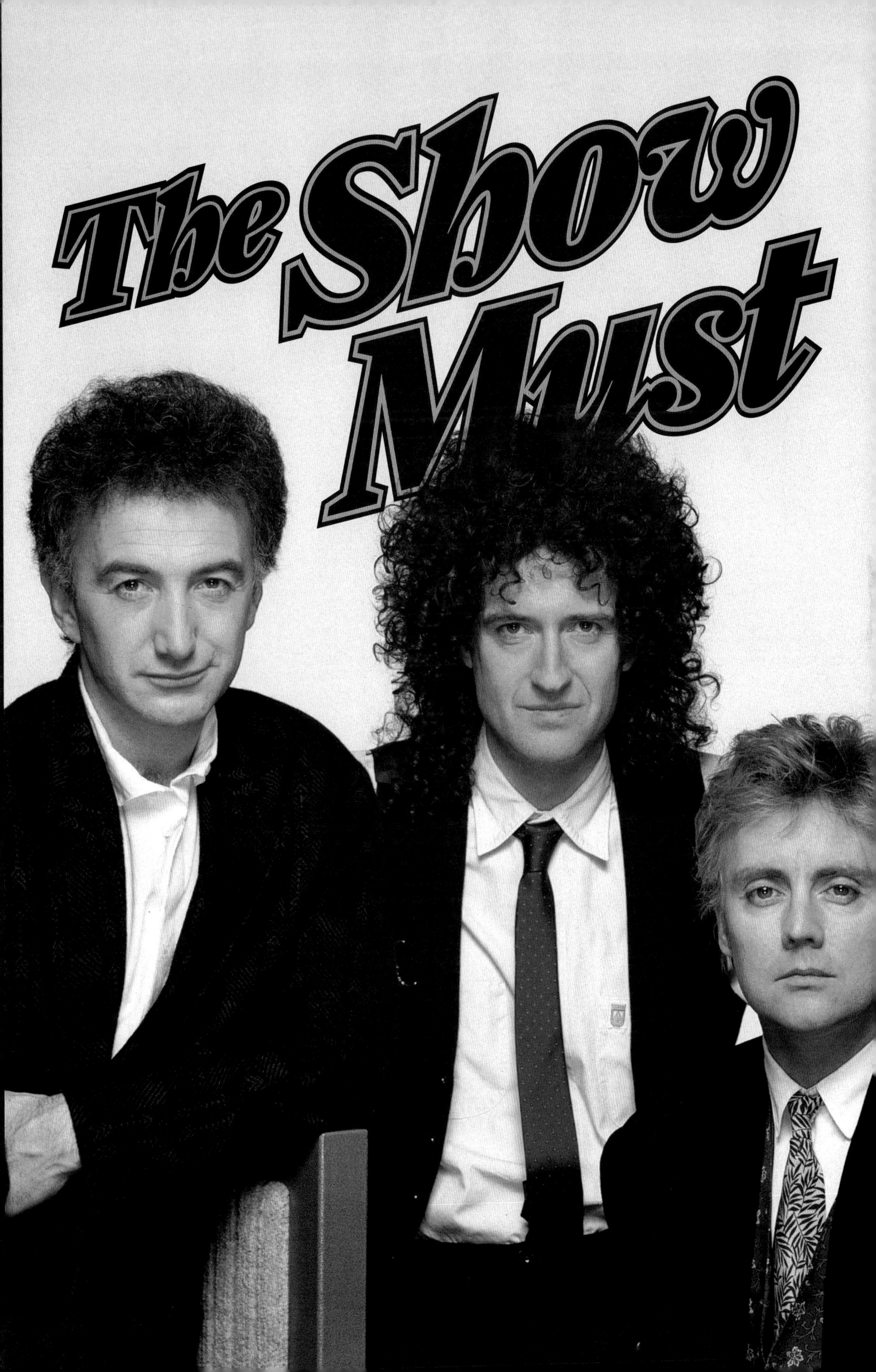
The Show
Must

GO ON...

BOWING OUT IN THE EARLY NINETIES: IT WAS TIME FOR MR MERCURY'S CURTAIN CALL

WORDS *Joel McIver*

As the Day-Glo Eighties rolled into the post-modern Nineties, Queen were fully embedded in the rock establishment. Like Phil Collins, Dire Straits, Rod Stewart and Eric Clapton, Freddie et al were now the face of the rich music elite, with slick suits, coiffed hair and fat investment portfolios – and although it's difficult to accept this if you're a Queen fan, the truth is that they were headed squarely into comfortable, unthreatening middle age.

We never got to see this happen, however. For Queen, or at least Freddie Mercury, the Nineties would only last two years.

Mind you, there was little sign that this mighty band's career would be curtailed at all, even at this late stage. In 1990, Queen switched record companies from Capitol to Hollywood Records, and in February that year, the four musicians made an appearance onstage at the Dominion Theatre in London to collect a BRIT Award for Outstanding Contribution to British Music. Sure, Freddie looked tired and allowed Brian May to do all the talking, but he'd been effectively absent from the press in recent years anyway, and most of us still thought that the rumours of his ill-health were just that – rumours. It never occurred to Queen fans that this would sadly be his final public appearance.

"We didn't know actually what was wrong for a very long time," said May, some time later. "We never talked about it and it was a sort of unwritten law that we didn't, because Freddie didn't want to. He just told us that he wasn't up to doing tours, and that's as far as it went. Gradually, I →

Some years later, Queen were awarded an undisclosed settlement for the sample as well as co-writing credits, not that this was likely to enamour May to hip-hop music. "I don't really relate to it, I have to say," he told Q. "I listen to 90 per cent of the rap records and I think 'What is this?' I'm just not in that world, you know. That doesn't mean it's rubbish, because a lot of people love it. I have kids, and they get into a lot of that stuff. Occasionally there's a little flash which gets to me, like Leila K and MC Hammer. I think Hammer's very cool: he has a great voice and great presence. The stars emerge, but the general run of it I don't understand, and I wouldn't pretend that I did."

Freddie rallied later in 1990, enabling Queen to write and record their 14th studio album, *Innuendo*, which came out early in 1991. As far as the press were concerned, everything was moving along as normal in the Queen camp, with May doing the bulk of the interviews as usual. Talking to *Vox* in January, he enthused: "I think *Innuendo* is the best [Queen album] for quite a long time. There's nothing I'm embarrassed about. Often you put out an album and you think 'But I wish we'd done this'. This one I feel quite happy about, and I can listen to it without any problems. I like it a lot. I think it's nicely complex and nicely heavy, and there's a lot of invention on there."

Asked if Queen would be touring any time soon, and knowing full well that Freddie was incapable of doing →

ABOVE The band celebrating their Outstanding Contribution win after the BRITs in 1990.

ABOVE RIGHT Mountain Studios in Montreux, Switzerland, had been owned by Queen since 1979.

OPPOSITE The BRIT Awards in 1990 was Freddie Mercury's last public appearance before his death the following year.

suppose in the last year and a bit, it became obvious what the problem was, or at least fairly obvious. We didn't know for sure."

Queen's music was very much in the public bloodstream in 1990, even in the absence of a new album, because the American rapper Vanilla Ice sampled the bass part from 'Under Pressure' and made it the basis of a massive hit, 'Ice Ice Baby', released in August. "I first heard it in the fan club downstairs," May told Q magazine the following spring. "I just

thought, interesting, but nobody will ever buy it because it's crap. Turns out I was wrong. Next thing my son's saying it's big here, and what are you going to do about it, Dad? Actually, Hollywood [Records] are sorting it out because they don't want people pillaging what they've just paid so much money for. We don't want to get involved in litigation with other artists ourselves, that doesn't seem very cool really. Anyway, now I think it's quite a good bit of work in its way."

❝ Freddie rallied later in 1990, enabling Queen to write and record their 14th studio album, *Innuendo* ❞

ABOVE (SEQUENCE) The video for 'These Are the Days of Our Lives' was shot in black and white to help disguise Freddie's declining health.

BELOW At the 1990 BRIT Awards, Brian gave the speech on behalf of the band when they picked up the Outstanding Contribution award.

so, May diplomatically said: "I love playing anywhere. If I go to places where other people are playing, I often get up and play myself. I just enjoy the sound and feel of playing, and I guess we don't do it enough as a band. That may change, but at the moment we're making albums and making videos, and touring worldwide."

Queen were also occupied at this time with reissuing their catalogue on CD, a commonplace practice for more or less any established band in the early Nineties. "We're releasing the back catalogue. It's been remastered digitally for the CDs," Roger Taylor told *Rockline*. "I think what the idea is, they're doing some real interesting remixes of our old tracks, like Rick Rubin has done a sensational remix of 'We Will Rock You'. It should be interesting."

"We're digging through the files to see if there's some of the old stuff that never got out that we can put on there," added May. "There are a few unreleased bits and pieces off our English radio appearances that might get on there. The only trouble is a lot of the tracks we rejected at the time ought to have been rejected. Sometimes you don't want to go back and fish out your garbage... there may be a few little gems that make it out there. We've been supervising the remastering onto digital of all those, every album that we ever made. It sounds so much better on the CD."

Between 13 and 16 May 1991, Freddie recorded his final Queen session in Montreux. These exact dates were the

> ❝ **Freddie would warm up his voice, request a shot of vodka and then say "Roll the tape"** ❞

subject of speculation for years, but they were finally confirmed by Justin Shirley-Smith, the assistant engineer for those sessions. Although May referred to this time as traumatic for obvious reasons, saying, "We all knew there wasn't much time left. Freddie wanted his life to be as normal as possible. He obviously was in a lot of pain and discomfort," Shirley-Smith added: "This is hard to explain to people, but it wasn't sad, it was very happy. He was one of the funniest people I ever encountered. I was laughing most of the time, with him."

According to May again, "For [Freddie] the studio was an oasis, a place where life was just the same as it always had been. He loved making music, he lived for it," and this proved to be the case, with a track, 'Mother Love', laid down successfully for future use. The singer, walking with a cane by then, and unable to sing more than a single verse at a time, would warm up his voice, request a shot of vodka and then say "Roll the tape."

After the sessions finished each day, the four musicians would have dinner

together; after the song was complete, Freddie announced he was returning to London "for a while". One more task remained to him – the filming of the video to accompany the next single, 'These Are the Days of Our Lives'. Shot in London by director Rudi Dolezal, the clip is a little painful to watch, as Freddie is so gaunt; still, he pulls off a subtly theatrical performance.

"AIDS was never a topic. We never discussed it. He didn't want to talk about it," said Dolezal some years later. "Most of the people didn't even 100 per cent know if he had it, apart from the band and a few people in the inner circle. He always said, 'I don't want to put any burden on other people by telling them my tragedy.'"

It emerged that Freddie was in fact in serious distress during the shoot. "The bottom of his foot was a completely open wound," explained Dolezal. "He must have had terrible pain, but you don't see that. You just see a man and his destiny. Regardless whether he was in pain or not, he always delivered. He

didn't want any special treatment. He was so brave. In retrospect, it would have been so easy to be a diva, but he wasn't like that."

The next single was 'The Show Must Go On', scheduled for release in autumn 1991 ahead of a new compilation, *Greatest Hits II*, but by then Freddie was too ill for a video shoot and so a clip was compiled of old footage. It's a glorious collection of film, featuring Freddie at his peacock-like finest, but the lack of a 'new' video inevitably caused yet more speculation about his health.

Greatest Hits II was a triumph, commercially speaking, when it came out in October. It became the tenth best-selling album in the UK, the seventh best-selling album in Germany and a diamond-certified seller in France, with 16 million copies sold worldwide. It certainly did better than *Blue Rock*, the third album by Roger Taylor's side project The Cross: released in mainland Europe but not in the UK as its predecessors had sold poorly, the album was overshadowed both by *Greatest Hits II* and the terrible news that rocked the world just after this point.

As October rolled into November, Queen fans looked ahead and wondered what their heroes' next move would be. A new album, perhaps? Or a tour, albeit limited if Freddie wasn't in the best of health? Surely he would recover soon, and the band would be back up to full strength.

That is, believe it or not, what we all expected to happen. ᛩ

INNUENDO

UK RELEASE DATE **FEBRUARY 1991**
HIGHEST CHART POSITION **1**
KEY TRACK **THE SHOW MUST GO ON**

The last true band album, *Innuendo* had a great deal of intelligent humour and pathos about it. Recorded at London's Metropolis Studios and the Mountain facility in Montreux, *Innuendo* was far too varied to be glibly cast as 'the AIDS album'.

In Queen's grand tradition, these 12 songs pinballed between genres – the title track alone offered vaudeville drum rolls, flamenco guitars and a screaming hard-rock solo from Brian May – and were inspired by themes as disparate as Taylor's cars ('Ride the Wild Wind') and Mercury's calico cat ('Delilah'). The effervescent 'I Can't Live Without You' and the foot-down 'Headlong' (a song originally mooted for May's solo career) hardly sounded like the work of a dead man walking.

"The last thing he wanted," said Roger Taylor of Freddie Mercury's defiant last stand, "was to draw attention to any kind of weakness or frailty. He didn't want pity."

Even so, at least three of *Innuendo*'s key songs offered a window into Mercury's mindset as the sand in the hourglass

Tracklist

1 Innuendo
2 I'm Going Slightly Mad
3 Headlong
4 I Can't Live with You
5 Don't Try So Hard
6 Ride the Wild Wind
7 All God's People

8 These Are the
  Days of Our Lives
9 Delilah
10 The Hitman
11 Bijou
12 The Show Must Go On

ran out. The singer's own 'I'm Going Slightly Mad' paired an itchy, haunted verse to a lighter chorus, with an incongruous Hawaiian slide-guitar solo and gallows humour metaphors that stopped the vocal from becoming too bleak ("This kettle is boiling over / I think I'm a banana tree").

Chiefly written by May – but with Mercury setting the lyrical tone and insisting that the bleakly ironic working title remained – 'The Show Must Go On' was darker still, led

as he looked deep into the lens for the whispered pay-off: "I still love you".

The feeling was evidently mutual, at least in the UK, where both the 'Innuendo' single and album reached No.1 without a sniff of promotion from the singer or the band setting foot on a stage.

The complex title track – which has been called the 'Bohemian Rhapsody' of the 90s and featured a guest

 In Queen's grand tradition, the 12 songs on *Innuendo* pinballed between different genres

by the doomy chop of strings and a wretched lyric ("Empty spaces / What are we living for?").

Sweeter – if no less affecting – was Taylor's 'These Are the Days of Our Lives', the drummer yearning for blissful formative years when "the bad things in life were so few". The gulf between those times and the here-and-now was starkly underlined by the single's monochrome video, with Mercury rail-thin and rooted to the spot due to the stubborn lesion on his foot, but still giving the performance his signature sparkle

appearance from Steve Howe – began as a jam, before being opened up into a flowing track that incorporated some fantastically synthesised orchestrations. Plus there's the arresting lyrics: "Surrender your ego; be free, be free."

Knowing that time was running out on their life as a recording band, the four members grouped together with the intention of creating something that rivalled the power of their most popular albums when they turned their attentions to *Innuendo*. They succeeded. ♒

Words: Henry Yates. Images: Getty Images, Shutterstock/Alan Davidson

The most important thing is to live a fabulous life. As long as it's fabulous I don't care how long it is.

Freddie Mercury

Who Wants to Live Forever

FREDDIE MERCURY'S TRAGIC
DEATH FROM AIDS IN 1991 DEALT A
SHATTERING BLOW TO ROCK'N'ROLL.
THIS IS THE STORY OF THE SINGER'S
ILLNESS, DIAGNOSIS AND LAST DAYS

WORDS *Henry Yates*

On 23 November 1991, Freddie Mercury finally shared the most open secret in music: "Following the enormous conjecture in the press, I wish to confirm: I have been tested HIV positive and have AIDS," ran the statement that the singer had dictated to Queen manager Jim Beach with some of his last breaths. "I felt it correct to keep this information private to date in order to protect the privacy of those around me. However, the time has now come for my friends and fans around the world to know the truth. I hope everyone will join with me, my doctors and all those worldwide in my fight against this terrible disease."

To those who had followed Mercury from his flamboyant first steps onto London's rock circuit to his reclusive final months, the news was shattering but grimly expected. After all, the peacocking Queen frontman had been the quarry of Britain's unregulated tabloid press for more than a half-decade, his health and sexuality the subject of ghoulish fascination and screamer headlines. No wonder that, years later, Brian May's protective fury was still palpable as the guitarist tore up a copy of the *Daily Mirror* on live TV.

The first whispers of a concealed illness had started as early as the summer of 1982, when it is alleged by authors Matt →

LEFT A message to Freddie from Elton John on the bouquet of roses he sent to the funeral.

ABOVE Freddie Mercury's funeral took place at the West London Crematorium and was conducted by a Zoroastrian priest.

OPPOSITE The singer is thought to have received his AIDS diagnosis in April 1987, but kept this information private until the end.

Richards and Mark Langthorne in their biography, *Somebody to Love: The Life, Death, and Legacy of Freddie Mercury,* that the singer had visited a New York clinic to assess a lesion on his tongue. Four years later, in October 1986, the British gutter press claimed Mercury had taken a blood test on Harley Street.

In the mid-80s, with HIV and AIDS treatments still in their infancy, diagnosis was a terrifying prospect. "Freddie knew about the virus appearing around the world, and knew of friends dying from the disease, so obviously that played on his mind," explained Mercury's personal assistant Peter Freestone. "He might have thought he was infected, but again, like many of us, he put it to the back of his mind, thinking, 'It won't happen to me'. You must remember, in those days it really was a death sentence."

Yet when the worst was confirmed in 1987, the singer's partner Jim Hutton told journalist Tim Teeman, Mercury did not crumble. "His attitude was 'Life goes on'. He took AZT [azidothymidine] and nearly every other drug available. The doctors came to the house to treat him. When he was diagnosed, he said to me, 'I would understand if you wanted to pack your

bags and leave'. I told him, 'Don't be stupid. I'm not going anywhere'."

Meanwhile, Freddie found that immersion in Queen's final albums could block out the gathering storm clouds. "The sicker Freddie got, the more it seemed he needed to record," remembered Roger Taylor in the *Queen: Days of Our Lives* documentary. "To give himself something to do, some reason to get up, so he would come in whenever he could. So really, it was quite a period of fairly intense work."

"[Freddie] just said, 'I want to go on working, business as usual, until I fucking drop'," added May. "'That's what I want, and I'd like you to support me in being able to do this, and that's why I don't want any discussion about this'."

Indeed, that late Queen material was the one medium where Mercury could face his plight, with the *Innuendo* album dropping several thinly veiled allusions, none starker than 'The Show Must Go On', with its ominous strings and lyrical foreboding ("Empty spaces / What are we living for?"). "We were dealing with things that were hard to talk about at the time," May told *Guitar World* in 1994, "but in the world of music, you could do it."

> 66 **Freddie found that immersion in Queen's final albums could block out the gathering storm clouds** 99

By the early 90s, though, the fans didn't need to study Queen's lyric sheet to know something was terribly wrong. It was hard enough to overlook Mercury's frailty as the band took the stage at the BRIT Awards of February 1990. By the time the lineup assembled for the music video to 'These Are the →

FAR RIGHT When the news of Freddie's death broke, fans came to pay their respects outside his Kensington home.

1 LOGAN PLACE
GARDEN LODGE

Days of Our Lives' in May 1991, even shooting in monochrome did little to disguise the singer's pinched cheeks and wasted frame.

"He knew how ill he was, and that this was the last time he'd ever be in front of a camera," director Rudi Dolezal told People. "The bottom of his foot was a completely open wound. He must have had terrible pain, but you don't see that. You just see a man and his destiny. Regardless [of] whether he was in pain or not, he always delivered. He didn't want any special treatment. He was so brave."

That winter, now almost blind and suffering mild fits, with his foot amputated and no strength to stand, Mercury settled at his home in Kensington's Garden Lodge, where he received a small circle of trusted guests at his bedside. "I have a house in London which wasn't too far from the house where Freddie spent the last few years of his life," remembered Elton John. "I didn't go and see him often because I found it really painful. AIDS was terrifying. He was physically terrifying to look at."

Smelling blood in the water, the sharks of the press hustled beyond the walls, hungry for scraps or perhaps the scoop of the decade. 'Top AIDS Docs See Freddie Mercury!' trumpeted *The Sun*. "How many more, Freddie?" chided the *Daily Star* in early November 1991, citing a "Russian roulette sex life likely to kill scores of his lovers". The same newspaper demanded the singer show his face: "Why are you hiding, Freddie?"

In the event, Mercury's statement was a masterstroke, defanging the tabloids by putting his illness in the public domain instead of on a red-top front page. And less than 24 hours later – having relinquished his medication a few weeks prior – the world's greatest rock'n'roll singer passed away, the cause of death officially cited as bronchial pneumonia. He died, reflected Mary Austin, "with a smile on his face".

"I was literally on my way to see him, less than half a mile away, when they rang me in my car and told me he had gone," Taylor told *The Big Issue*. "I stopped the car on Kensington High Street, in a kind of shock [...] I just wish I'd got to say goodbye."

"I think Roger and I both went through a kind of normal grieving process but accentuated by the fact it has to be public," May told Smooth Radio. "Losing Freddie was like losing a brother."

Fewer than 40 guests attended Mercury's modest funeral service in West London, where a Zoroastrian priest performed the ceremony. And while the singer once joked that "I want to be buried with all my treasures like Tutankhamun", that day his coffin crept into the crematorium flames to the strains of Aretha Franklin's 'Take My Hand, Precious Lord', before the ashes were entrusted to Austin, who swore never to reveal their location. "He didn't want anyone trying to dig him up," she told the Mail Online.

Even now, furious at being gazumped, the tabloids bared their teeth, running stories that suggested Mercury had died of his own sexual perversions. "He was sheer poison," wrote Joe Haines in *The Daily Mirror*. "A man bent – the apt word in the circumstances – on abnormal sexual pleasures, corrupt, corrupting and a drug taker. His private life is a

LEFT George Michael joined Queen to perform '39', 'These Are the Days of Our Lives' (with Lisa Stansfield) and 'Somebody to Love'.

LEFT MIDDLE David Bowie and Annie Lennox performing 'Under Pressure'. The star-studded concert also featured Metallica, Def Leppard, U2 and Elton John to name a few.

LEFT BOTTOM The event raised money for the Mercury Phoenix Trust, which helped fund AIDS research.

revolting tale of depravity, lust and downright wickedness."

"I find it unconscionable," reflected James Rogan, director of *Freddie Mercury: The Final Act*, in an interview with Pink News. "There were headlines like, 'I'd shoot my son if he had AIDS'. You'd read it and think: 'How did this manage to make it into print?' I just can't get my head around it."

Thankfully, the wider world was kinder. From the moment the news broke, flowers from Queen fans festooned the pavements outside Garden Lodge, while the farewell messages scrawled on the property's walls led *Time Out* to declare the location "London's biggest rock'n'roll shrine" (until new owner Austin was finally forced to clean the walls in 2017 following complaints from neighbours).

Meanwhile, the rock industry demanded its own goodbye. Held at Wembley Stadium on 20 April 1992, The Freddie Mercury Tribute Concert for AIDS Awareness underlined the late star's status in the rock'n'roll firmament, with a stellar lineup paying musical tribute while kick-starting

Queen's new charity, the Mercury Phoenix Trust. As May hollered from the stage: "We're gonna give him the biggest send-off in history!"

But when the dust settled, the survivors of Queen found themselves facing an unknowable and unsettling future. Releasing his own statement that "it is impossible to replace Freddie", bassist John Deacon walked away from the Queen setup and took up the reclusive existence he maintains to this day. As Taylor reflected in *The Show Must Go On* documentary, he couldn't see a road ahead either. "It was an odd period. Really, the band was over."

As for May, he told Virgin Radio, "In my mind, it just seems like there cannot be a Queen without Freddie" and that "my role now is to be me". But as he set out alone with 1992's solo album *Back to the Light*, the guitarist recognised that his world – personally and professionally – had shattered. "Apart from the grief of losing someone so close," he noted, "suddenly your whole way of life is destroyed. All that you have tried to build up for the last 20 years is gone…"

MADE IN HEAVEN

UK RELEASE DATE **NOVEMBER 1995**
HIGHEST CHART POSITION **1**
KEY TRACK **IT'S A BEAUTIFUL DAY**

In terms of sales figures alone, there could be little doubt that the Queen hardcore – and more than a few fairweather fans – approved of this posthumous album that featured vocal and piano parts recorded by Mercury in the months before he died.

Put together as a labour of love by Queen's surviving members, *Made in Heaven* was released on 6 November 1995, and topped the UK album chart, marching towards multi-platinum sales and spitting out five Top 20 UK singles.

Stripped of context, few connoisseurs would argue this was the strongest album in Queen's auspicious catalogue. But there were moments here well-worthy of the brand, including the neck-tingling opening salvo of 'It's A Beautiful Day', the title track's rousing balladry and the impossibly moving 'A Winter's Day'.

"The last album is one of the most ridiculously painful experiences, creatively, I have ever had," Brian May told BBC Radio 1. "But the quality's good, partly because we did

Tracklist

1 It's a Beautiful Day
2 Made in Heaven
3 Let Me Live
4 Mother Love
5 My Life Has
  Been Saved
6 I Was Born
  to Love You
7 Heaven for Everyone
8 Too Much Love Will
  Kill You
9 You Don't Fool Me
10 A Winter's Tale
11 It's a Beautiful Day
   (reprise)
12 Yeah (hidden track)
13 13 (hidden track)

have those arguments. Whether it's healthy for life or not is another matter."

Curiously, given the praise shortly to be heaped onto The Beatles' cut-and-shut 'Free as a Bird' single, press reaction to

things, I will sing, I will sing. And then you do what you like with it afterwards and finish it off'."

By completing *Made in Heaven*, the Queen survivors had fulfilled their leader's last will and testament in the band's

" The Queen survivors had fulfilled their leader's last will and testament in the band's inimitable style "

the album was somewhat muted, with *NME*'s memorably virulent review focused on the ethics of the project ("*Made in Heaven* is vulgar, creepy, sickly and in dubious taste"). In truth – and whatever your take on the album's musical merits – anecdotal evidence all points to the fact that this last hurrah was exactly what Mercury had hoped for in Montreux.

"Freddie at the time said, 'Write me stuff, I know I don't have very long,'" explained May in the *Queen: Days of Our Lives* documentary. "'Keep writing me words, keep giving me

inimitable style, rather than leave it to industry vultures to crudely reanimate and repackage the sweepings. Perhaps just as important, they had exorcised the demons and drawn a line under the original band's extraordinary first run. As May remembered of the process: "You were just listening to Freddie's voice 24 hours a day and that can be hard. You suddenly think, 'Oh God, he's not here, why am I doing this?' But now I can listen to *Made in Heaven* and it's just joy – and I feel like it was the right album to finish up on…" ♛

Words: Henry Yates Images Getty Images

CHAPTER 6
- *Legacy* -

IS THIS THE REAL LIFE? IS THIS JUST FANTASY?

6

QUEEN *Forever*

POST-FREDDIE, QUEEN
TOOK THEIR OWN ADVICE
ABOUT 'KEEPING YOURSELF
ALIVE': IT'S WHAT HE
WOULD HAVE WANTED

WORDS *Joel McIver*

QUEEN

What do you do when you lose a friend who is also the face of your internationally known rock band? You pay your respects, you take the time to heal – and then you ask yourself a series of very big questions.

The thoughts running through the heads of Brian May, John Deacon and Roger Taylor as 1991 became 1992 would have been "Is Queen over whether we like it or not? If not, do we *want* it to be over? If not, will Queen work without Freddie?" or words to that effect. For two of the musicians, the answers were clear: one of them was less sure, as we'll see.

Just as Vanilla Ice had given Queen's popularity an unexpected boost with his frankly silly song 'Ice Ice Baby' in 1990, the *Wayne's World* movie did much the same when it was released in early '92. Produced before Freddie's death, but coinciding by chance with the wave of public grief that accompanied his loss, the film

did more than most of us realise for Queen's legacy – thanks to its classic, and genuinely funny, scene of four metalheads headbanging to 'Bohemian Rhapsody' in the back of a car.

The song, reissued in January as a charity release, reached Number 2 on the *Billboard* Hot 100 for five weeks – revealing, if anyone was in doubt, that Queen and their music were very much part of the public conversation. Interest in the group's next move was soon at an all-time high.

As a result, 1992 turned out to be a busy year for Queen, with recognition at the MTV Video Music Awards, a compilation album called *Classic Queen* reaching Number 4 in the USA – and, of course, the Freddie Mercury Tribute Concert at London's Wembley Stadium on 20 April. Only eclipsed in concert terms by the previous Live Aid and subsequent Live 8 and Live Earth events, the show was an emotional, star-studded rollercoaster that anyone

BELOW John Deacon played with Queen a handful of times in the 90s before retiring.

ABOVE Paul Rodgers performed with Queen between 2004 and 2009.

RIGHT Queen were awarded a star on the Hollywood Walk of Fame in 2002.

> **With *Made in Heaven*, Queen fans were both thrilled and saddened... It was surreal to hear Freddie singing on his final recordings**

brand. May did release his first solo album, *Back to the Light*, in 1992, and Taylor issued his third LP, *Happiness?* two years later, but both performed respectably rather than spectacularly, fans understanding that these were essentially side projects to tide them over until a new Queen album appeared in some form or other.

When this arrived in 1995 in the form of *Made in Heaven*, Queen fans were both thrilled and saddened. It's a decent collection of songs, but it was genuinely surreal to hear Freddie singing on his final recordings in 1991. It reached Number 1 in the UK with ease, selling 20 million copies worldwide: its function was really to close off Queen's 25-year Mercury era in style, and it fulfilled that role admirably.

There was a period of hiatus for Queen at that point, with the musicians' focus elsewhere, although in 1997 they recorded a song called 'No-One But You (Only the Good Die Young)', dedicated to Freddie for obvious reasons, while promoting a new best-of album, *Queen Rocks*. The

over 40 will remember watching in awe. Over a billion people watched it on TV, and over £20 million was raised for AIDS research thanks to the unique bill, featuring the three Queen musicians playing alongside Elton John, David Bowie, George Michael, Annie Lennox, Seal, Def Leppard, Robert Plant, Tony Iommi and Roger Daltrey, as well as members of Guns N' Roses, Extreme and Metallica.

After this phenomenal tribute to their fallen comrade, it made sense for the three musicians to take some time out, and indeed it was a further three years before any serious stirrings of activity were felt from the Queen

same year, they performed 'The Show Must Go On' with Elton John and the Béjart Ballet in Paris, an emotional moment for all involved, and in the case of John Deacon, the perfect moment to bow out permanently.

The truth is that after Freddie's death, Deacon seemed to have lost all desire not just to be in Queen, but even to be a regular working musician. He has never said much on the subject apart from "There is no point carrying on; it is impossible to replace Freddie" to *Bassist* magazine, and he simply doesn't do interviews any more. Even May and Taylor barely deal with him these days, the odd business-related email aside.

Most of us might find it tricky to sink into obscurity after the adulation Queen received, but Deacon seems to have mastered the fine art of doing very little. He likes holidaying in the French resort of Biarritz and playing golf, according to Queen's fanclub magazine, but otherwise he's a family man with six children.

What Deacon has actually done as a musician since '91 is as follows. After the 1992 Tribute Concert, he played with Genesis and Pink Floyd at an EMI private party. In '93 he played a fundraiser with Taylor to raise money for the King Edward VII Hospital in London, and then in 1995 he performed a guest spot with the Spike Edney All Stars, a bunch of Queen session →

RIGHT American singer Adam Lambert has toured and performed with Queen since 2011.

musicians, at London's Shepherd's Bush Empire.

After the events of 1997, Deacon basically vanished. He didn't even turn up when Queen were inducted into the Rock & Roll Hall of Fame in 2001. Media interest in him has been relatively subdued in the interim, although the occasional image of him out and about doing everyday things has surfaced.

There was one slightly juicy story in 2002, when Deacon was pictured enjoying the company of a semi-naked pole dancer, said to be named Emma Shelley. The pictures are still available online but they're not particularly flattering; they just show a faintly knackered-looking bloke in his fifties admiring a nearby woman. Nothing official was said on the subject by Deacon, Shelley or anyone else, although the tabloids got into a froth – and that, it seems, is that.

May and Taylor could have followed Deacon into comfortable retirement if they'd chosen. In 1997 the former was 50 and the latter 51, and they'd paid their dues on a thousand flights and tour buses over a quarter of a century: in their position, we suggest that many of us would have retreated to our country mansions to spend some quality time with our immense personal fortunes. However, the two remaining Queen members took the opposite route, building not one but two new phases of the band – as follows.

The first few years post-Deacon were spent in legacy mode, as management companies put it. In 1998, they performed 'Too Much Love Will Kill You' with Luciano Pavarotti at a benefit concert organised by the Italian opera singer, also playing 'Radio Ga Ga', 'We Will Rock You', and 'We Are the Champions' with the pop star Zucchero. In '99 they released the patchy *Greatest Hits III*, a jumbled mixture of singles, remixes, live stuff and curios like a rapped version of 'Another One Bites the Dust' with Wyclef Jean. A major box set called

> ❝ **The two remaining Queen members took the opposite route, building not one but two new phases of the band** ❞

The Platinum Collection came out the following year and was a much better compilation, eventually going seven times platinum in the UK and five times platinum in the US.

The first signs of new musical activity came in 2003, when May and Taylor played at the 46664 Concert hosted by Nelson Mandela in Cape Town, to raise awareness of HIV and AIDS in South Africa. This led to re-recordings of old Queen songs with modern singers, such as a Robbie Williams-sung version of 'We Are the Champions', and was the first time that the 'Queen +' concept was used. This was an excellent way of extending the Queen brand while honouring their new collaborators and – importantly – paying respect to Freddie and John: simply moving on as 'Queen' would undoubtedly have angered the purists in their still-huge fanbase.

The first collaboration was, improbably, with Mandela himself: a new song called 'Invincible Hope' included a speech by the great statesman and was released as Queen + Nelson Mandela on the *46664: One Year On* EP in 2004. This was followed the same year by the formation of a much grander concept, the touring band Queen + Paul Rodgers, with vocals supplied by the former singer of Free and Bad Company. Rodgers first sang with May and Deacon at their induction to the UK Music Hall of Fame, and proved immediately that he could handle the job with aplomb: indeed, he is one of the very few singers of Freddie's age who could do so.

A successful world tour, Queen's first since 1986, followed in 2005 and '06, taking the new band through Europe, Japan and the USA. The new concept was met with open arms by public and critics alike, ushering in a new phase of the group's career in a way that had not really been seen since AC/DC replaced their late singer Bon Scott with Brian Johnson all the way back in 1980. Bands rarely change lead singers with any degree of success, but in the case of Queen, the switch was made in fine style.

The new group was welcomed both by the rock'n'roll establishment and by a new wave of rock bands, a good example being when Queen received the first VH1 Rock Honors in Las Vegas in 2006. The Foo Fighters played 'Tie Your Mother Down' at the start of the ceremony before jamming on a series

of Queen songs with the musicians themselves. It's interesting to note that the Foo Fighters, perhaps the biggest rock band in the world as we write this in 2022, combine much of the passion and scale of early to mid-career Queen in their own music.

Momentum continued for Queen + Paul Rodgers, who released an album called *The Cosmos Rocks* in '08 to more or less positive reviews. It's a solid rather than seismic record, but its function was really to kick-start another round of touring rather than to wow anyone with its creativity, and in that sense it was a success. The band's second and last world tour was a monster, including a show in Kharkiv, Ukraine in front of 350,000 fans that was filmed for DVD, as well as sold-out gigs in Moscow, London's O2 Arena and Buenos Aires.

In 2009, Queen and Paul Rodgers shook hands and called it a day, although both parties left the door open for future collaborations. Their partnership had been phenomenally successful, giving both band and singer a latter-day career boost – but more importantly, showing the world that Queen could perform perfectly well on the strength of their catalogue, even in Freddie's absence.　　　→

MIDDLE Queen first performed with Adam Lambert while the latter was competing on *American Idol* in 2009.

ABOVE At the closing ceremony for the 2012 London Olympics, Queen were joined by Jessie J on vocals.

Images Getty Images

> **It was instantly apparent that Adam Lambert had something – a certain extrovert panache, perhaps – that fitted with Queen's songs**

LEFT From one Queen to another: Brian and Roger on stage for the Platinum Party at the Palace in June 2022.

ABOVE Lambert has received widespread critical acclaim for his performances with Queen.

One more time, May and Taylor could quite easily have retired at this point. Instead, they took the Queen + concept to a whole new level – by recruiting a singer from a completely different demographic to the veteran blues-rocker Rodgers. This time, they found a man who might as well have been the living reincarnation of Freddie himself.

The first time that Queen played with Adam Lambert was on 20 May 2009, when they performed 'We Are the Champions' on the season finale of the TV talent show *American Idol*. For that

broadcast, the winner Kris Allen and the runner-up Lambert sang a duet, and it was instantly apparent that the latter had something – a certain extrovert panache, perhaps – that fitted with Queen's songs. Older than most people think (he was 27 at the time), Lambert was neither too youthful to deter Queen's older fans, nor so old that a new generation of kids wouldn't like him.

It was two years before a further collaboration occurred, but Queen had plenty to be getting on with in the meantime. Another compilation, this

time called *Absolute Greatest*, came out in 2009, and May and Taylor performed 'Bohemian Rhapsody' on *The X Factor* alongside the finalists of that year's show. Behind the scenes, the group walked away from EMI after a 40-year partnership, signing to Island Records, which then reissued all 15 previous Queen albums in 2011.

The same year, Queen received the BMI Icon Award for their radio success in the US and a Global Icon Award at the MTV Europe Music Awards: you may well ask yourself which other bands formed in 1970 were still getting such plaudits. At the latter ceremony, Lambert joined May and Taylor for 'The Show Must Go On', 'We Will Rock You' and 'We Are the Champions' – and the set proved so popular among viewers and fans that it was obvious that the collaboration should continue.

As indeed it did: from that point on, the Queen + Adam Lambert band has been a regular live fixture worldwide, and is now into its second decade as a stadium-filling group. Live dates around the world in 2011-12 wound up with a show-stopping set featuring Jessie J at the closing ceremony of the Summer Olympics in London. In a nod to Freddie's fans, Queen showed a video clip of the late singer performing his famous 'Day-Oh' call and response routine.

After this high point, it's easier to pinpoint places where Queen + Adam Lambert *haven't* toured than where they have. Highlights have included Las Vegas in 2013; the US, Australia, New Zealand and the Big Ben New Year concert in 2014; and across Europe and Asia on the Queen + Adam Lambert 2016 Summer Festival Tour. A giant

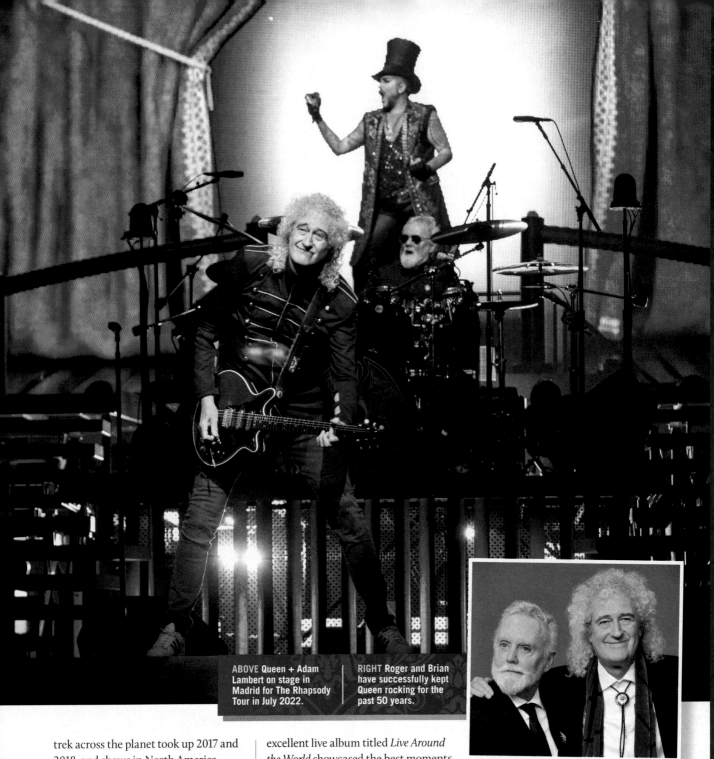

ABOVE Queen + Adam Lambert on stage in Madrid for The Rhapsody Tour in July 2022.

RIGHT Roger and Brian have successfully kept Queen rocking for the past 50 years.

trek across the planet took up 2017 and 2018, and shows in North America, Japan, South Korea, Australia and New Zealand took them through 2019 until the start of the pandemic, when they downed tools like everyone else.

Have May and Taylor recorded albums with Lambert? Indeed they have, but perhaps wisely, new songs have been sparse compared to renditions of the classic material. A 2014 studio album called *Queen Forever* featured three new songs, using old vocal tracks from Freddie, and another inclusion was a duet with the late Michael Jackson called 'There Must Be More to Life Than This'. In 2020, an

excellent live album titled *Live Around the World* showcased the best moments from more than 200 shows by the new band, and is probably the best souvenir of the Queen + Adam Lambert collaboration available.

And they're still not done. In June 2022, the band played the Platinum Party at Buckingham Palace in honour of Queen Elizabeth II's Platinum Jubilee: you may remember the late monarch and a CGI Paddington Bear tapping teaspoons on cups to the beat of 'We Will Rock You'. Finally, as we write this anyway, Queen's 1989 album *The Miracle* was given the box set treatment at the end of '22, a highlight being

the inclusion of a previously unheard song, 'Face It Alone'. It's an affecting, anthemic song that leaves the listener gripped – and as such, is just what Freddie would have wanted.

Raise your glass to Queen, folks. Brian May and Roger Taylor could have followed Freddie, and then John, away from the music industry, not once but twice. Instead, they knuckled down, rebranded the band and gave their fans what they want and deserve most – the chance to hear that unbeatable catalogue of songs. For that, we salute them. ♛

THE SHOW MUST GO ON

Queen + Adam Lambert performing The Crown Jewels shows in Las Vegas, September 2018. "You give Adam the job and there's nothing that guy can't do," May explained in an April 2022 interview with *Forbes*. "He can handle all the old Queen catalogue. And not imitating Freddie – doing his own thing."

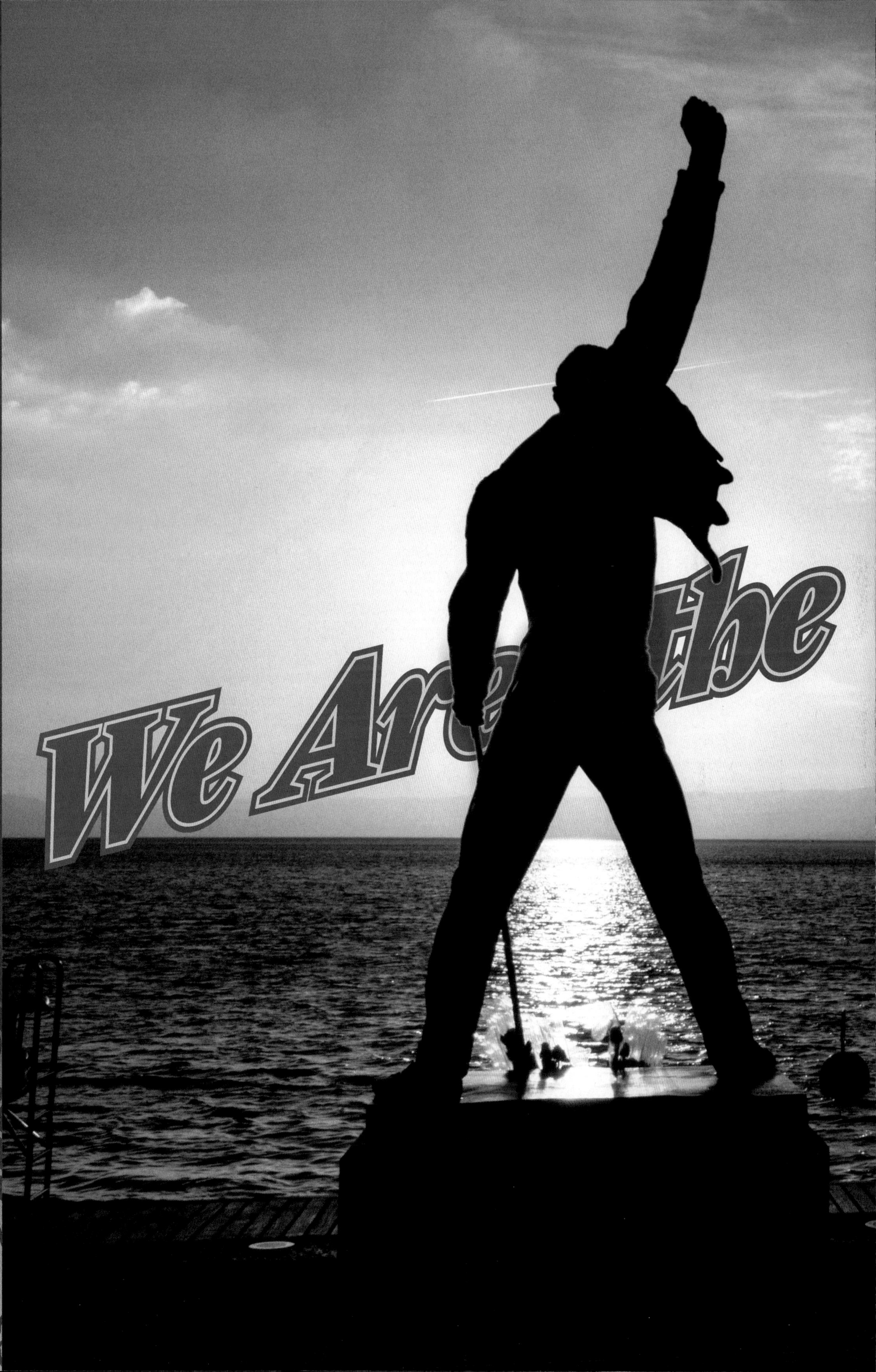
We Are the

Champions

QUEEN HAVE RESHAPED AND
REDEFINED ROCK MUSIC FOR
MILLIONS OF FANS: WE'LL
REMEMBER THEM THIS WAY

WORDS *Joel McIver*

The sheer numbers associated with Queen are enough to blow anyone's mind. Even back in 2005, the venerable *Guinness Book of World Records* told us that their albums have spent a total of 1,322 weeks on the UK album charts, a period of time which is better understood as 26 years. That's right – an entire human generation. More up-to-date sources tell us that in 2022, their *Greatest Hits* collection from 1981 is not only the sole album that has shifted over 7 million copies – in other words, one in ten Brits has it – but it is also the best-selling album in UK history. Even *Greatest Hits II*, a relative newcomer from 1991, has become our country's tenth-biggest seller, with sales of over 3.9 million copies.

As for America, where Queen were believed to have completely blown it in 1984 with the outrageous video for 'I Want to Break Free', *Greatest Hits* has spent over 500 weeks – a decade! – on the chart. As recently as 2018, the US magazine *Business Insider* stated that Queen are the third most popular rock band of all time in its country, after fellow British acts The Beatles and Led Zeppelin. Maybe the importance of that   →

conservative-baiting music video has been a little overstated?

You take our point. Queen are a phenomenon of massive proportions. They've had 18 Number 1 albums, 18 Number 1 singles, and ten Number 1 DVDs worldwide, selling somewhere between 250 million and 300 million units, however they may be defined. They're the only band inducted into the Rock & Roll Hall of Fame in which every member has written more than one Number 1 hit, and they were given a Grammy Lifetime Achievement Award in 2018.

Now, a group doesn't get that big, over such a long period of time – 50 years and counting, remember – without making a serious musical impact. The list of modern bands who claim a Queen influence reflects the variety of music that they played, particularly in the Freddie era: in the rock arena, look no further than The Darkness, Foo Fighters, Muse, Jane's Addiction, The Smashing Pumpkins and The Killers for evidence of Queen's glamorous, seductive, theatrical approach.

In the world of heavy metal – a style of music, by the way, which Queen played with great humour and enjoyment – take a look at the over-the-top musicianship and stage shows of Guns N' Roses, Iron Maiden and Dream Theater. Don't forget the biggest metal band of all – Metallica – who embraced Queen with a ferocious cover of 'Stone Cold Crazy'.

In the world of pop music, if you want to know where Freddie's preening, hugely extrovert stage persona hit home, see the early work of the late George Michael and his successors Robbie Williams, Scissor Sisters and Lady Gaga. Finally, even bookish intellectuals such as Radiohead have found inspiration in Queen, with that band's singer Thom Yorke picking up the guitar after seeing Brian May perform on TV.

Beyond mere music, Queen meted out a cultural transformation too. They are said to have been the first Western rock act to be officially accepted in Iran, while their songs have been heard as rallying cries in South Africa's

ABOVE Freddie Mercury's performance style has been an inspiration for countless artists.

Images Getty Images, Alamy

LEFT The musical *We Will Rock You* became an audience favourite.

BELOW LEFT The futuristic musical was written by Ben Elton (centre).

BELOW As British icons, Queen appeared on several commemorative postage stamps.

> **Freddie Mercury has been a beacon of encouragement for performers of a wide range of sexual preferences and gender identities**

Purple are currently still touring – even then, with only one founder member remaining – while Led Zeppelin and Black Sabbath called it a day in 1980 and 2017 respectively. This is primarily down to three things: their continued tours with Adam Lambert, the long-running *We Will Rock You* musical, and the *Bohemian Rhapsody* movie, all of which provide a solid reason to imbibe a dose of Queen in different ways.

Let's look at the musical first. Written by the comedian and author Ben Elton, *We Will Rock You* is a convoluted vehicle for a large number of song performances, encapsulated in a story that has strong science-fiction influences: Elton mentioned *The Matrix* films as an inspiration when the production opened in 2001. Rarely has a stage production divided the critics and the public so clearly in the years since then: *We Will Rock You* is one of the longest-running stage shows in West End history, with audiences queuing up to see it, but it received savage reviews when it launched.

The Guardian wrote that the concept "really is as sixth form as it sounds", while the *Daily Mirror* wrote that "Ben Elton should be shot for this risible story" and the *Daily Telegraph* scoffed that the show was "guaranteed to bore you rigid". Still, we doubt that Queen and Elton gave a damn about the reviews when the production proved to be a long-standing success.

As for the triumphant *Bohemian Rhapsody* movie? We should note, first of all, that its title was a masterstroke in a way that – say – *The Mercury Story* or *Killer Queens* would not have been. Without Freddie as the face of the band, Queen and their management have tended to zero in on their biggest song to represent them. You don't have to be a Queen fan to know that there is a song called 'Bohemian Rhapsody', associated with an image of four faces on a black background, and that people tend to jump around in excitement, playing air guitar, when it comes on the pub jukebox. Your postman knows it, your neighbour knows it, your grandmother knows it – so Queen exploiting the →

Black communities. Furthermore, as a bisexual man – although he remained more or less private about that fact in his lifetime – Freddie Mercury has been a beacon of encouragement for performers of a wide range of sexual preferences and gender identities, an important part of today's conversation, especially in the music industry. In 2009, a poll of 5,000 people included him on a list of most popular gay icons, and as for the delicious campness of his live performance style, which modern live performer *hasn't* adopted some of that approach on stage in recent years?

The fact that Freddie died so young of AIDS, which claimed many thousands of lives before effective therapies were introduced, also shone a powerful light on the disease. The 1992 Tribute Concert played a role in making it clear that AIDS affects everyone, not merely a small sector of the population, and the Mercury Phoenix Trust continues the mission. To this day, Freddie is the most prominent celebrity to have lost his life to this terrible virus. What else might he have achieved, had he not died three or even four decades before his time?

As a band, Queen are still very much here, unlike so many of the class of 1970. Of their contemporaries, only Deep

TOP LEFT Joseph Mazzello, Rami Malek, Gwilym Lee and Ben Hardy as John, Freddie, Brian and Roger in 2018's *Bohemian Rhapsody* biopic.

ABOVE & LEFT Brian performing 'Love of My Life' with a recording of Freddie at the 2019 Global Citizen Festival in New York.

widespread awareness of 'Bohemian Rhapsody' in the title of their 2018 film was only the logical thing to do.

Unlike the *We Will Rock You* musical, *Bohemian Rhapsody* was a commercial *and* critical hit. Written by Anthony McCarten, produced by Graham King and Queen manager Jim Beach, and directed by Bryan Singer, the film revolves around the startling performance of the American actor Rami Malek as Freddie. Indeed, the movie is really Freddie's life story as opposed to the story of Queen the band, although May, Deacon, Taylor and their orbiting friends, family and colleagues are portrayed faithfully. The timeline of the movie begins with Freddie's teenage years, when he was still known as Farrokh Bulsara and enduring racist misery as an airport baggage handler, and takes us through to Live Aid in the summer of 1985. The remaining

six years of Freddie's life are not addressed, with the film-makers wisely opting to finish at the peak of his – and Queen's – career.

Although *Bohemian Rhapsody* was a success, recouping 18 times its $50 million budget with a phenomenal return of over $910 million, and scooping four Oscars, a Golden Globe and a BAFTA award, its history was troubled. The film was originally announced all the way back in 2010, with Sacha Baron Cohen attached to the main role: most people understood that Baron Cohen would have made a good Freddie, although he was a little too tall for the part. Funnily enough, Rami Malek was slightly too small to be a perfect match for the singer, although this didn't detract from his performance. Baron Cohen soon walked away, while Bryan Singer also came and went as director, leading to a final co-directing job for Dexter Fletcher,

although he was eventually credited as executive producer.

Still, the movie industry is always chaotic, and it's a mark of the tenacity of all involved that such a good film was made. Once the enormous grosses made by the movie were revealed, production companies scrambled to get in on the music biopic market. *Rocketman* and *The Dirt*, the stories of Elton John and Mötley Crüe, were released in 2019; Aretha Franklin's *Respect* came in 2021; Baz Luhrmann's astounding *Elvis* came in 2022, as did the TV series *Pistol*, based on Sex Pistols guitarist Steve Jones' memoir. Whitney Houston's big-screen biopic, *I Wanna Dance with Somebody* – also from *Bo Rhap* writer Anthony McCarten – is due at the end of 2022.

What are we left with? A band that changed everything they touched, largely for the better. Queen are among the most acclaimed groups that ever existed, and the number of trophies

LEFT Rami Malek won an Oscar for his portrayal of Freddie Mercury.

BELOW As of July 2022, Queen's *Greatest Hits* remains the UK's best-selling album of all time.

> "Queen are among the most acclaimed groups that ever existed"

on their collective mantelpiece is now immense. It's been a long way since 1974, when *Sounds* voted them third Best New British Band and *Disc* said they were the 10th Brightest Hope: May and Taylor must chuckle at that one nowadays. Their first Band of the Year award came from *Melody Maker* in 1975, and songwriting honours began to flow in the same year – an Ivor Novello here, a Golden Lion there.

After the 'Bohemian Rhapsody' single, it was game on for awards, with dozens landing on Queen's doormat in the late Seventies. By 1984 they had received charitable recognition from Nordoff-Robbins Music Therapy and elsewhere, and many video awards came in once music TV became the dominant medium. The rest of Queen's awards list is far too long to repeat here.

In the interests of balance, we should note that when a band becomes as embedded in a nation's cultural fabric as Queen have – even being invited to play for the real Queen several times – they can reasonably be accused of having lost whatever edge or threat they once had. We know how gleefully confrontational Queen were in the Seventies, after all, and we also know how comfortably they meshed with the establishment from the mid-Eighties onward.

The counter-argument to that accusation is that, even in 2022, Queen continue to surprise us. No-one expected this band to be still touring at this stage in their careers. No-one could reasonably have expected a perfect partner for them like Adam Lambert to appear. And no-one would have thought that they could single-handedly kickstart a movie biopic industry that shows no sign of losing steam. This is a band with a vision. One vision... ♛